SINISTRAM

A NIGHT VIGIL NOVEL: BOOK THREE

GAIL Z. MARTIN

CONTENTS

SINISTRAM
A NIGHT VIGIL NOVEL: BOOK THREE

By Gail Z. Martin

eBook ISBN: 978-1-64795-092-7
Paperback ISBN: 978-1-64795-093-4

SOL Publishing is an imprint of DreamSpinner Communications, LLC

CHAPTER ONE

"BEHIND YOU!"

Travis Dominick shouted a warning. A shotgun boomed seconds later as his partner, Brent Lawson, wheeled and sent a blast through the ghost that appeared from nowhere a few feet away.

Rock salt sent the spirit packing with an angry wail.

"Guess we've met the ghost who's been causing trouble." Brent kept the shotgun up and his finger on the trigger. "Mark the sigils. I'll watch your back."

Eighty years ago, Michael Poole fell to his death from one of the towers at the Durable Cement factory. The facility had once been a booming concern, only to wither and die as markets and manufacturing changed. Now abandoned, the large site had fallen into disrepair, attracting thrill seekers and legend trippers who explored modern ruins and went looking for spectral trouble.

"Third tower," Travis reminded Brent. "At least, that's where they found the body."

"Lead the way."

Storms and vandals had taken their toll over the years. Taggers had covered the walls with graffiti, garbage collected in the corners, and most of the windows were broken. Travis picked his way across the debris-littered ground, careful of his footing while he kept watch for Poole's ghost—or other spirits—to appear.

Cement making had been dangerous work. Aside from the usual hazards of falls and heavy equipment, wet cement burned skin, and the dust caused fatal lung damage. Poole wasn't the first to die on the job at the old factory, but he had been the last fatality before it closed.

Locals suspected that the actual death counts were doctored by management, and old-timers claimed to know people who had been paid to keep quiet about a family member's on-the-job death back in the day.

For years, the dead kept their silence. But lately, something had roused ghosts like Poole's from uneasy sleep. People who lived near the old plant or drove by it daily started reporting seeing jumpsuit-clad gray figures at the edges of the property and its access roads. That caused more than one accident, which is how Travis and Brent ended up on the job.

Travis kept a flask of salted holy water in his left hand and blessed chalk in his right. When he reached the tower, Brent took up his position as guard while Travis chalked sigils to banish ghosts and demons, dispel evil, and remove negative energy.

He could sense the ghosts watching them, but for now the spirits kept their distance.

"Hurry up, the energy's building," Brent said.

Travis took a deep breath, and his right hand went to the silver crucifix hanging from a chain around his neck. He left the priesthood years ago, but had never forsaken his vows to heal, guide, and protect.

"Spirits of the dead, hear me." Travis's measured tone was both commanding and reassuring. "Your time here is over. You were wronged and died too soon, but the people responsible are long dead. It's time to move on. There is no one for you to take your vengeance on."

The wind stirred, colder than before. Travis felt the hair on his arm rise and a prickle at the back of his neck.

"You've got their attention," Brent said. "Finish up so we can get the hell out of here."

"I would ask that you leave by your own accord, but you can't continue to harm the living. Go now, or I will send you to your final rest," Travis continued.

The wind picked up, and Travis could hear the sound of distant, angry muttering. Then invisible hands pushed him backward, nearly making him lose his footing.

Brent fired the shotgun into the empty space where the shove had originated, and for a few seconds, the air lightened, until more ghosts rushed in to make their displeasure known.

"They aren't listening!" Brent shouted, as if Travis hadn't noticed.

The wind swept toward them again, but this time it carried a fine cloud of white dust, billowing across the debris-strewn factory yard.

"Try not to breathe," Travis cautioned. "Cement dust is bad news."

"I'll keep that in mind," Brent replied as they both pulled respirators from their backpacks.

More ghosts appeared like shadows in the dust, far more than the company claimed. Apparently, they were done waiting.

Travis pivoted into the exorcism litany, as useful against hostile ghosts as demons. *"Exorcizamos te, omni immundus spiritus..."*

Poole's ghost howled in fury, and the dust swirled around them, making it difficult for Travis and Brent to see. Scowling faces appeared in the cloud reaching out for them with grasping spectral hands. Scratches appeared on their faces and arms, proof that the ghosts could do real harm.

"Plan B. On my mark." Travis spoke a few words of magic, and the wind pushed the cloud back toward the tower where Poole had fallen on the other side of the yard.

"Now!"

Brent fired his shotgun into the billowing dust, igniting it in a fireball around the old tower.

"Run!" Travis had gone a few paces before he realized Brent wasn't behind him, still keeping his gun trained on the cloud of spirits. He ran back and grabbed Brent by the arm. "Come on!"

They nearly made it to the gate before they heard a thunderous crack and the old tower split, collapsing as the flames engulfed it.

Much as Travis wanted to stop and catch his breath, he knew that they needed to be long gone before the police showed up. He and Brent piled into his old Crown Victoria, a car he chose because of its powerful engine and enough room in the trunk for a body. Travis didn't burn rubber, but he got them back on the main road headed in the opposite direction in record time. They pulled off their masks and shoved them under the seat.

"Talk to me. Can you breathe? Are you okay?"

Brent nodded. "Yeah. Although if we get stopped, we're probably covered in cement dust. You are, so I'm betting that I am too."

Travis glanced at the rearview mirror. "Shit. There's a box of wipes under the seat. Maybe we can at least clean up enough not to get noticed."

Brent laughed as he reached for the box. "And we'll smell 'powder fresh.'"

"Shut up." Travis could tell from his reflection that his grin had the slightly maniacal 'we lived through it' edge that came with cheating death.

Travis was thirty-four and six-foot-two, with solid lean muscle, chin-length black hair, and green eyes. The cement powder in his hair and eyebrows made him look like he had suddenly aged decades.

Not too very long ago, Travis had been a member of a secretive order of warrior priests who used magic and arcane knowledge from the Vatican archives to fight demons, malicious hauntings, vampires, and other infernal creatures, the Sinistram. The Sinistram reported to Cardinal Vasylyk, one step away from the Pope, and considered itself to be the "left hand" of the Holy Father, fighting the monsters in the dark.

Not all of the Cardinals approved of the Sinistram's secrecy, hubris, or tactics. They called the organization by another name: *Filios Tenebrarum*. The Sons of Darkness.

Internal politics, corruption, and cynicism led to Travis's highly controversial resignation from a role that was supposed to be for life. He left the Sinistram, left the priesthood, and left the Church, although the Sinistram refused to accept his decisions and made periodic "invitations" to return, which Travis always rebuffed in no uncertain terms.

Instead, Travis now ran the St. Dismas Outreach along with his helpers, Matthew and Jon, a halfway house in a rough part of Pittsburgh that served the homeless and fought paranormal dangers on the side. Named for the believing thief on the cross, it gave a wry nod to the protecting and healing parts of his past vocation that Travis had never renounced.

He drove them back to Brent's office on the South Side.

"Do you think that will stop the hauntings?" Brent asked as they parked, and Travis followed him inside.

"Hope so, although Poole certainly wasn't the only fatality," Travis replied. "Dangerous work is one thing, but cutting corners on safety features is evil."

"Happens every day."

"Doesn't mean I have to like it," Travis said.

Brent's office was in a converted house, so it had a full bathroom where they could shower, handy in a line of work that often left them covered in dirt, blood, and gore. Travis usually left clean clothes at the office for just such occasions.

"Go ahead and get the first shower. I'll make a fresh pot of coffee and see if we've got cookies." Brent waved Travis ahead of him.

Brent was in his early thirties, with short blond hair and a muscular build. His first brush with the supernatural came when demons killed his parents and his twin brother, Danny. He barely escaped a demon attack that claimed most of a village when he was in the military, causing painful injuries that flared up at the worst times.

Angry and ready for revenge, Brent swore he would find a way to avenge his family and atone for surviving.

Now, Brent was ex-military, ex-FBI, and ex-cop, finally opening a private detective agency that specialized in paranormal cases. That put his supernatural experience to good use and addressed problems that regular law enforcement wasn't prepared to handle. It also gave Brent more schedule flexibility on days when painful old injuries from the military or demon hunting caused problems.

Like Travis, Brent had seen enough corruption, denial, and cronyism to be disillusioned and angry, but he was too stubborn to abandon what he thought of as his core mission: stopping the things that went bump in the night.

Travis had met Brent on a case where they were both hunting the same demon and decided to team up. It wasn't like the television shows about fearless monster hunters, which Travis and Brent were fond of watching to poke fun. Nights like tonight reminded Travis how much fiction and reality differed.

Travis took a quick shower, letting the hot water sluice over him, making sure the dust didn't clump since he had no desire to try to get cement out of his hair. He breathed deeply, letting the delayed reaction of mortal terror drain away as his heartbeat slowed to normal.

Monster hunting wasn't a career choice with a retirement package. More like penance, not so different from making a vow to a holy order or swearing allegiance to an army. But as he and Brent often remarked over coffee or a "glad-we're-still-alive" beer, it was a dirty job someone had to do, and they were uniquely qualified.

The vision came on suddenly, between one breath and the next. *He saw a concrete entrance into a hillside with huge steel doors. The doors swung open of their own accord, but it was too dark to see inside. In the next breath, all-consuming fire obliterated the entrance and the hillside.*

"Hey, leave me some hot water!" Brent banged on the bathroom door, only partially in jest. "I'm too old for cold showers."

"What? Can't hear you!" Travis tried to buy himself time to get his thudding heart under control.

"Fucker," he heard Brent mutter. Travis turned off the water and toweled off.

Visions weren't new to Travis. He had glimpsed snippets of the past, present, and future all his life. No matter how baffling they seemed when they first appeared, they usually turned out to be related to something he was struggling with in the present. Right now, Travis couldn't imagine any connection to the fiery scene he had just witnessed.

He dressed quickly, threw his clothes in a plastic grocery bag to take back to the mission, and checked his hair one last time for cement before relinquishing the bathroom.

"All yours," he said as Brent passed him on the way in with a stack of his own clothing. "Are there cookies?"

"I even left some for you," Brent teased. "And if you drink all the coffee, make more." He closed the door in Travis's face, laughing.

Travis went out to the office lobby, which had once been a living room, and helped himself, sitting on the couch to wait for Brent. In the time they had been working together, the two loners had forged a solid friendship and trusting partnership, something Travis was grateful for but still found remarkable. Since their efforts were mistrusted as vigilantism by regular law enforcement, which didn't openly acknowledge the existence of the paranormal, that bond mattered a lot.

"I left most of a pot for you," Travis said when Brent joined him, still toweling off his wet hair.

"Alex is due to make a supply run, so running out isn't really a problem," Brent replied. "Cookies, coffee, pain killers, first-aid supplies, salt in the big industrial-sized container, and whiskey."

"Sounds like what Matthew orders every week, except for the whiskey." Travis didn't have any issues with alcohol and often joined Brent for a drink, but out of respect for the halfway house residents who struggled with sobriety, he didn't allow any on the property.

Brent raised his coffee cup in salute. "Cheers." He shoved a cookie in his mouth and took a couple of swallows before giving a satisfied sigh.

"I don't want to tempt fate, but we both got out of there fairly unscathed. That's a rarity," he observed.

"Don't jinx us," Travis cautioned. "Do you need me to bless some more holy water while I'm here?"

"Sure. Thanks. Comes in handy." Brent ate a second cookie and washed it down.

"Does it seem like the ghosts have gotten more aggressive lately? Almost like they're provoking a fight?"

Travis hummed in agreement with a mouthful of coffee. "Yeah, and there's nothing to account for it—full moon, religious holiday, death anniversary. You think C.H.A.R.O.N. is doing something to cause it?"

Brent grumbled several uncharitable epithets. "Maybe. Maybe not, but I'm happy to blame them anyhow."

C.H.A.R.O.N., which stood for Central Handling Arcane Relics and Occult Networks, was an elite, secretive paramilitary organization of demon hunters who tried and failed repeatedly to recruit Brent, whose distrust ran deep. Travis and Brent had just run up against CHARON on their last big case, proving that the organization hadn't cleaned up its act or improved its ethics.

"Could just as easily be Sinistram," Brent pointed out.

"True," Travis allowed. "Although juiced-up local hauntings are small fry for them. They like the big world-ending, cackling villain apocalyptic shit."

"Tell me how you really feel," Brent teased.

Travis shrugged. "You asked."

"And maybe it's just a run of bad luck." Brent brought over coffee and cookies. "Not everything that happens at the same time is related."

"Cause and effect can be hard to see without a bigger picture. Not that I want more attacks, but we need more data points." Travis took a bite of cookie and washed it down with the java. He needed a hit of sugar and caffeine to get a second wind.

"We can contact the other hunters we know in the area," Brent suggested. "See what they're hearing, and if things have been busier than usual in their neck of the woods. It could just be a coincidence. But if it isn't...I'd rather catch it early."

"I'll make some calls too," Travis said. "What's your calendar like tomorrow? Want to go have a look at the Darr Mine—speaking of spirits acting badly."

"Nothing I can't shift around," Brent answered. "Do you think the problems are random, or connected?"

"Won't know until we look into it. Could go either way." Travis refilled his cup and poured more for Brent while he was up.

"How deserted is it? Can we go in daylight, or do we have to sneak in at the dead of night?"

"It's out near Van Meter, not too far from here. The mine entrance is closed, and the area is pretty grown over," Travis replied. "It's still the worst coal mining disaster in Pennsylvania history, even though it happened back in 1907. Which is saying something because there were two other big disasters that same year, one in Pennsylvania and one in West Virginia. If something supernatural was feeding off death and destruction, it sure got its fill."

"How many died?" Brent leaned back and finished his cookie.

"Two hundred and thirty-nine," Travis said. "The explosion got blamed on miners carrying open lanterns in an unsafe area, but the bosses never took responsibility for that kind of thing," he added with a bitter note. "Although they did stop using that kind of lamp afterward."

"Bully for them," Brent replied.

"Some of the bodies were never recovered. The ones that were brought out were so badly burned they could only be identified by the clothing," Travis went on. "They weren't buried at the mine, but there's a memorial marker. The mine never reopened."

"I'm guessing that families took their dead for local funerals if they could identify them, and the others were buried in a common grave," Brent said. "Probably done quietly, but there's got to be paperwork somewhere. Maybe they were buried on the mine property itself, since it no longer functioned?"

When Travis didn't respond right away, Brent looked at him with concern. "Are you okay? You seem a little spooked."

Travis shrugged. Brent knew about his visions, but admitting one always left Travis feeling vulnerable. "I caught a glimpse of something, and I don't know what I saw."

"Something...like a vision? Think it's connected to the mine we're going to?" Brent asked.

"Don't know. It didn't match any of the photos or drone footage of the site that I've seen," Travis replied. Unknowns were dangerous, and he didn't like loose ends.

Brent listened quietly while Travis described his vision. "Too bad your woo-woo doesn't come with a time stamp," Brent said. "At least you didn't see either of us getting Kentucky-fried."

"Just keep it in mind," Travis told him. "It's bound to show up somewhere."

"Will do."

"I don't begrudge the miners their revenge, but why now? Like tonight, the people who did them wrong are long gone. What's given them the mojo to start attacking people who just happen by at the wrong time? It's been over a hundred years. Seems odd for them to just wake up and raise hell," Brent pointed out.

"Guess it's our job to find out." Travis gave Brent an assessing once-over. "You okay from the fire? Need to have Matthew check you out?"

Brent shook his head. "No burns. I checked when I showered. Didn't get hit with anything. All in all, I'm in good shape, compared to how it usually goes."

"Me, too," Travis agreed. "I'll head back to St. Dismas and get some work done, make some calls. Then we can meet up in the morning and go over to the mine. Sound good?"

"Deal."

———

TRAVIS WASN'T SURPRISED that Matthew was still up when he got back to St. Dismas. He and Jon were sitting in the lobby, savoring cups of hot chocolate, trying not to look like parents waiting for an errant teen to come home after curfew.

"Am I grounded?" Travis joked, although he appreciated having people watching out for him.

"That depends," Jon said with mock seriousness. "Do you deserve to be?

Jon was a former Army chaplain, five-foot ten and forty-something, built like a fireplug with short-cropped dark hair, wary eyes, and chestnut skin. Matthew was ex-Army, like Brent. That unspoken bond had helped Brent to accept the medic's services more than once, although it was a language Travis didn't share.

"You wouldn't happen to know anything about that fire at the old cement factory, would you?" Matthew raised an eyebrow.

"Maybe." Travis didn't try to prevaricate. Both of the other men knew about the monster hunting and seemed to understand that it was part of Travis's self-imposed absolution.

"Did it work? And where's Lawson? He usually needs patching up," Matthew replied.

"Surprisingly, neither of us took more damage than some scrapes and scratches." Travis poured a hot chocolate for himself from the urn on a nearby table and took a seat with them. "Although I can't say the same for the factory."

He recounted their adventure without any dramatic flourishes, since reality was dangerous enough.

"You were lucky that you didn't get blowback with the fire and scorch your lungs," Matthew chided.

"And yes, we could have been incinerated. But we weren't."

"This time," Jon said.

"Hey, it worked. That should mean no more ghosts killing the locals." Travis didn't mind their mother-henning, but felt compelled to defend himself.

"Good point," Matthew conceded. "But we also want you and Brent to remain among the living."

"Much appreciated." Travis took a sip of hot chocolate and savored the warmth and taste, ignoring the sudden craving for a shot of Kahlua. "How's the house tonight?"

"Nearly full," Jon replied, knowing Travis meant St. Dismas. "More than usual for a nice night. Glad we can help, but I'm sorry so many folks need it."

"Those contributions from the antique shop in Charleston and the ghost tour company in Cape May came through," Jon said. "Please tell your friends, 'Thank you.'"

"I will." Travis and Brent had gotten to know others with supernatural skills who also helped fight off paranormal predators. Some of those friends had become regular donors to St. Dismas, which Travis deeply appreciated.

"And I know you probably had your phone ringer turned off all night, but check your messages," Jon added. "Your friend from Conneaut Lake called looking for you, so it must be important."

Travis reached for his phone, unlocked it, and saw that his one and only message was from Mark Wojcik, another monster hunter who covered territory north of Pittsburgh.

"Hey, Travis," Mark said. "Hope you and Brent are alive and kicking. I know it's a drive to Franklin, but there's a wake tomorrow for Al Saunders. Don't know if you ever hunted with him, but he's one of ours, and he got taken out by a rougarou. Strange circumstances. I'll explain when I see you. Let me know, and I can text directions. Thanks."

Travis had played the message on speaker. He looked at Jon and Matthew after it ended and checked his watch. It wasn't too late to return the call, at least, not by hunter standards. "Guess I'd better find out what's going on."

Mark picked up on the second ring.

"Thanks for returning my call." His voice sounded scratchy, but whether it was from the weather or whiskey, Travis couldn't tell.

"No problem. I didn't know Al personally, but I heard him mentioned on the hunter grapevine. Sorry to hear he passed. A rougarou? Seriously?"

He knew that particular type of monster had to hit hard for Mark. A wendigo killed several members of Mark's family, getting him into the monster-hunting life and breaking up his marriage.

"I hate to sound more paranoid than usual," Mark said with a bitter laugh, "but I think there's more to it."

Travis frowned. "What do you mean?" It was a joke among hunters that being paranoid didn't mean things weren't out to get you, something that proved true more often than not.

"I can fill you in if you and Brent come up, but the short version is I think something is hunting the hunters."

Travis exchanged a glance with Jon and Mathew. "Say what?"

"Al is the third hunter in as many months just in my corner of PA," Mark said. "None of the guys who died were rookies or thrill-seekers. Two of them had been at it longer than I have, because they showed me a trick or two back at the beginning. Al had been hunting longer than any of us, but he wasn't old, and he wasn't slow. He was one of the craftiest bastards I ever met, so if something got the jump on him, it wasn't normal, even for us."

"Anyone piss off a coven lately?"

"Not to my knowledge. That's just it...they could be coincidences, but my Spidey sense is telling me there's more to it," Mark replied. "If I were the superstitious type, I'd blame it on the black moon."

Travis knew enough about astronomy to know that meant the second new moon in a month. Some people considered it to be an omen. He had learned long ago to trust intuition, even from people who didn't have his psychic or medium abilities. Hunters who went with their gut tended to live longer than those who played by the book.

"Okay. Text me the time and place, and I'll let Brent know. I'll get a room for the night so we can do the wake right and not have to drive back to the city."

"Father Leo is going to do the service. He went on several hunts with Al over the years," Mark said.

"Thanks for letting us know. I hope you're wrong..."

"So do I. But I'm really afraid I'm not. See you soon." Mark ended the call, and a moment later, his text came through with directions. A quick call to Brent gave a condensed version of what Mark said and gained agreement to meet early and drive up together.

Travis put down his phone and looked to his friends. "Well? I know you're thinking something."

"On top of Brent's suspicions that something is stirring up the ghosts and creatures around here, it's worrisome," Matthew said.

"We just did a smackdown with CHARON not long ago. I would have thought it would take longer for them to get their mojo back," Travis said.

"Sinistram?" Jon asked.

Travis tried not to squirm at the thought. "In the past, they couldn't be bothered with local hunters. Or hauntings and monsters that didn't come with world-ending curses. I can't imagine why they would care now—changing their minds didn't come easy."

When he spoke of the Sinistram, it was always "they." Never "we." Travis had left that life behind and wanted as little to do with it as possible, but the small world of supernatural protectors meant crossing paths was inevitable.

"Sorry to run out on you again." Travis felt a flash of guilt, although he knew his duties were more than adequately covered.

"Goes with the calling, if not the job." Jon shrugged. "We'll be fine. And maybe when you get back, before you hare off on the next hunt, you could drop in at the Sinistram library, just to take the temperature."

As an inducement to return, the Sinistram permitted Travis access to their secret arcane library, a privilege usually reserved for members of the Order. He went when there was no other choice to research a case, but between the thinly-veiled censure for leaving and the open pressure to return, the experience was never enjoyable, even if it proved productive.

His expression must have made his unspoken thoughts clear, because Jon and Matthew chuckled.

"Your face is saying the quiet part out loud, Travis," Jon laughed. "Tell us how you really feel."

Travis rolled his eyes. "You've heard me whine before. Sinistram gives me access, then piles on the guilt for not coming back."

"You're Catholic and they're an arm of the Vatican," Matthew said. "Of course they do."

Travis shot him the bird. "Still. It's less of a courtesy and more of a recruitment tactic. I'm clearly the prodigal son."

"More like the one who got away," Jon remarked. "You're a damn fine hunter, and you've proven by stopping a couple of potentially world-ending problems that you can do just fine without them. That has to sting."

"Yeah, well," Travis grumbled. "They're everything people complain about with the Church. Stuck in their ways, close-minded, judgmental, and hypocritical. They want me for my abilities, but they also want me to feel guilty and damned for having those abilities. Fuck them."

"And yet...we still serve," Matthew pointed out with a glance up at the painting of St. Dismas.

"I look at it as family trauma," Jon said. "Can't live with it, can't live without it."

"They've never revised their views on immortal creatures who repent doing harm and change their ways," Travis grumbled. "Once a monster, always a monster, and we know that isn't true."

"It's not just the Sinistram that has trouble with that idea," Matthew said. "So do plenty of hunters."

No one questioned the need to stop feral, unreasoning monsters that attacked out of instinct, hunger, or malice and could not be tamed or made less of a threat. Likewise, the need to deal harshly with people who used magic to kill or cause harm was widely accepted. The gray area fell with those supernatural creatures like vampires, weres, and other reasoning beings who weren't actually human.

"Back in the old days, they had special cloisters for those who wanted to withdraw to avoid temptation," Matthew recalled. "It was always a question whether the choice to enter those cloisters was voluntary. At best, they were a refuge. At worst, a prison based solely on having paranormal abilities."

"Which was better than nothing, I guess," Travis agreed. "But the uprising in 1659 burned the cloisters and killed everyone assigned there," he reminded them. "Which just made everything worse."

"That's not just the Church, it's human history in general," Jon said. "As a species, we fuck up a lot."

"Amen," Matthew muttered. The conversation lagged, and they sat in silence for a few moments.

Finally, Travis finished his hot chocolate and stood. "I need to get some sleep. I can't say I'm looking forward to the wake tomorrow, but maybe Brent and I will find out something that helps explain what the hell is going on."

"And it slows you down from going right back out to look into that haunting at the Darr Mine, like you intended," Jon added.

"I guess a day won't hurt too much," Travis conceded. "But it's another case where a long-ago disaster that hadn't caused problems in a long time suddenly flared up."

"It'll still be there the day after tomorrow," Matthew assured him. "Now get some rest."

Travis said goodnight to his companions before he took his cup to the kitchen and headed to his room.

He set out his clothing and checked the supplies in his go-bag before he changed for bed. Travis always wore several silver protective saints' medallions, day and night, and kept a rosary in his jacket pocket, along with a flask of salted holy water.

Travis considered which weapons might make the most sense at the mine. He had some altered flash-bangs that could spread salt, powdered silver, and iron flakes, and make a nice little explosion with a loud noise. He tossed in a couple, mindful of being careful that igniting them wouldn't cause a bigger fire.

He always carried silver knives in addition to his Glock with silver bullets and a shotgun with rock salt rounds. Matthew kept him provisioned with essential field medicine supplies, and Travis confirmed that he hadn't depleted his stock. When he felt sufficiently prepared, he set the bag aside and turned out the lights.

Mark Wojcik's words repeated in Travis's mind as he lay in bed, staring at the ceiling, unable to fall asleep. Brent believed something had stirred up long-dormant haunts and turned them dangerous. Mark was convinced that something was hunting the hunters. The two seemed contradictory.

Could both be true, with different entities behind them? he wondered.

More frequent, powerful manifestations endangered the general public, but particularly hunters, who took it upon themselves to stop paranormal threats from harming civilians. Increased confrontations automatically created more opportunities for hunters to get hurt or killed doing their job.

If someone or something was intentionally targeting hunters, the end result was the same.

Hunters didn't recruit new hunters. Broken people found their way into hunting after something supernatural killed people they loved, and they went looking for vengeance. That was true for everyone Travis knew who was "in the life," as hunters called it. There was no central hunting organization, no formal education, and no union. Hunters learned from each other, formed friendships and loose alliances, and took care of their own, like with Al's wake.

Take out too many at a time, and replacing them will take a while.

That could leave a gap unless folks come in from other areas. But people tend to stick to the region they're from, for a lot of reasons, Travis mused. *They know the territory, the legends, and sometimes, the cops. They've got side gigs or day jobs. Hard to pull up stakes.*

If the spike wasn't a coincidence, then the question was, what entities were powerful enough to make it happen? CHARON was the most likely candidate, since they were aggressively anti-monster, but playing a long game wasn't their style. *Too subtle.*

The possibility remained that an unknown coven or powerful witch might be manipulating the situation for their own ends, either to get rid of hunters they viewed as a threat, or to make the surviving ones more hard-line.

Possible, but seems like a stretch.

Which left Sinistram, an option Travis still considered unlikely. Sinistram's cadre of specially trained "ninja" priests with arcane abilities considered home-grown hunters to be armed rabble, but didn't object to using them for cannon fodder.

Sinistram complains about hunters, but they'd actually have to work more without them. They like feeling superior, but I can't see them siding with the monsters against humans. What's in it for them? They're a secret organization, so they aren't going to get famous. They're funded by the Vatican, so they don't need money. That leaves power—over whom? To do what?

We're missing pieces, and I'm afraid this is going to bite us on the ass if we're not careful.

The day's activities were finally catching up to him. Travis yawned, trying to get comfortable. He wondered whether he would get another vision, something to make sense of what he had seen.

Let's see what Brent and I can pick up at the wake and get from Mark. Maybe if we all compare notes, someone will have the pieces the others are missing.

But we'd better figure it out soon. These things always have a short timeline, and the clock is already ticking.

He fell asleep in the wee hours of the morning, and while he did not have any visions, his dreams were restless.

CHAPTER TWO

"THANK YOU FOR COMING. I know it's a drive," Mark Wojcik welcomed them when they arrived for the wake. He shook their hands firmly and clapped them on the back.

Mark was about Brent's height and build, solid and strong from his day job as a mechanic, with blond hair and green eyes. He was usually quick with a joke, so it seemed strange to see him so subdued when they weren't on a hunt.

"Thank you for letting us know. I wish we were getting together under better circumstances," Brent said, and Travis echoed the sentiment.

"I don't know how many of these folks you know." Mark walked in with them from the parking lot. "I can introduce you. They're hunters, so don't expect much in the way of social skills."

The memorial service for Al Saunders was short and ecumenical, held in the back room of Fletcher's Bar. What was left when the rougarou was done with him had already been cremated and buried in a corner of a local cemetery that hunters had quietly claimed for their own.

A donated headstone was promised to show up the next week,

bearing only his name and dates. He had no family, except for the other men and women who shared the danger, burden, and nightmare of their calling.

Brent counted fifteen men and two women, ranging in age from early thirties to late fifties, all in flannel shirts, canvas jackets, worn jeans, and boots—practical gear that transferred from hunting deer to stalking monsters. The women looked as hardened as the men and stood together off to one side.

Father Leo spotted them and came over to shake hands, since Mark had introduced them on a hunt a while back. "Travis and Brent. Good to see you. Thanks for coming. I'm guessing Mark's already shared his thoughts?"

Brent nodded. "And we're hoping to get to talk privately after the service. Sorry about your loss."

Father Leo Minnelli still looked youthful at nearly forty, with wavy brown hair and brown eyes. He was the chaplain of St. Gemma Galgani, a rural church that served a few dozen families in a sparsely populated area that had seen better days. Aside from those duties, he worked with the Occulatum, another group of monster-hunting priests that weren't as hard-assed as the Sinistram. He was in between Travis and Brent's heights, with a trim build that suggested he kept in shape.

Leo hadn't left the priesthood, but he had made it clear at their first meeting that he bore Travis no ill will for his choice.

"There are all kinds of monsters," Leo had said back then. *"Addiction, family trauma, loneliness. This way, I get to make a difference with both kinds."*

"Definitely. You're staying the night at Mark's?" Leo asked.

Travis nodded. "He had room, and we figured it gave us more time to talk."

"Good. We need to find some answers. I've done too many services like this lately," Leo replied.

Fletcher's looks like a hunter bar, Brent thought. Mounted buck heads with impressive antlers decorated the walls between dart boards and Steeler pennants. The television over the bar was dark now, and the bottles of hard liquor beneath it didn't bother with top-shelf brands, just the cheap painkillers that helped get patrons through the night. Classic road trip hits from the seventies played in the background.

If someone knew where to look, there were protective sigils carved into the scarred old bar, and Brent was willing to bet a trench filled with salt encircled the building. A silver amulet hung from a chain around the buck's neck, one that Brent recognized from his own selection of charms. He felt certain that the other hunters all wore some variation just as surely as they carried salt and silver bullets. Everyone was armed. Concealed carry was a way of life up here.

"Don't recognize you boys," an older man said, after Father Leo moved on. "How'd you know Al?"

Brent guessed the stranger was old enough to be his father, with the grizzled look of someone who had seen things they would never be able to forget.

"We did a hunt with him and Mark a while back," Travis fibbed, since it was easier than explaining and none of the man's business. "Done a number of jobs with Mark and Father Leo. They asked us to come, and we came."

"Humph. You're not from around here." The statement carried layers of meaning and more than a little judgment.

"Not all monsters stay in their territories." Travis drew on the easy charm that made him good at questioning witnesses. "We lend a hand when we can."

"Ah, well. If Wojcik and the Padre vouch for you, that's good enough. God knows, we need as many hunters as we can get. Seems like there are fewer every day." He cleared his throat. "I'm Bob."

"Nice to meet you. I'm Travis, and this is my hunting partner, Brent." Travis was quiet for a moment. "Father Leo sounded like your area's been hit hard lately."

Bob took a swallow from his beer, although it was still morning.

Most of the hunters in the back room also held cans, bottles, or glasses, fortification for the memorial. "Don't know if the monsters got smarter or we got slower, but it's been a rough patch, that's for sure."

"Anything else change?" Travis inquired gently.

"Not so anyone's figured a connection," Bob replied. "Believe me, we've looked. Maybe Jupiter is in retrograde or something screwy like that."

A bell rang, silencing the chatter and focusing attention on Father Leo, who stood at the back of the room. He wore a black liturgical stole but otherwise had not donned vestments. A photograph of a man, Brent assumed to be Al, sat on the shelf behind him, but there were no other religious decorations, although the bar's music had been turned off.

"Thank you for coming out to say farewell to Al Saunders, a friend, neighbor, and a damn fine hunter," Father Leo said. "He protected this area from evil and gave his life in service. There is no higher praise."

Everyone raised their drinks in tribute as Leo continued.

"We pray for his soul, that he finds peace and safety in the arms of our Lord, where all God's creatures exist in harmony beyond the reach of harm and evil."

"Amen," rumbled through the crowd. This wasn't a group for flowery sentiment. Brent bet that most, if not all, of the hunters had military or law enforcement backgrounds like his own, moving from fighting one kind of threat to another, an ingrained need to protect and serve.

Father Leo removed the stole and carefully wrapped it up before stashing it in his backpack. A few hunters moved forward to speak to him in quiet voices. The rest of the hunters regrouped in threes and fours, nursing their beers. Mark moved from one group to another, short conversations that might have been questions or condolences. Brent figured Mark would catch them up later, in private.

"What's the deal with Fletcher's?" Brent asked when Mark rejoined them.

Mark sipped from his can of Iron City. "It's been here close to fifty years, so I'm told. The story I got is that the original owner lost a son to a werewolf and offered a bounty to anyone who could kill the creature. Somebody did, and brought the head in for proof. Ever since, it's been the place hunters gather where they know they're welcome. Other folks too, but they know the deal."

Brent had to admit that he envied their community, just a little. "You're lucky. A lot of hunters are solitary types and not very friendly."

Mark shrugged. "The hunters here come from all over this neck of the woods. Mercer, Meadville, New Castle, and beyond. There's a lot of open territory and plenty of woods, plus lakes and streams. Handy for the creatures, but hard for us to track them down. We're pretty good about working together when we need to. Only get a couple of fist fights, now and then," he admitted.

Once the memorial was over, the hunters began to drift away until only Brent, Travis, Mark, and Father Leo were left. Father Leo poured out a measure of whisky in respect for Al in the yard outside while Mark ordered burgers to go for all of them, and they followed him back to his house.

"It's not anything exciting, but it's home," Mark said as they joined him at the door. The cozy, well-maintained log cabin sat at the end of a dirt road.

Mark paused before he opened the door. "Don't forget, Demon and Donny will be happy to see us."

Brent remembered to brace himself an instant before two large, dark, furry shadows burst out of the house. One he recognized as Demon, Mark's Doberman. The other he guessed to be Donny, a derpy werewolf who had become one of Mark's best friends.

"Good boys," Mark greeted the onslaught, ruffling Demon's fur and patting Donny on the head. "Such good boys. Did anyone come by the house? Did you eat any intruders? Such good boys."

Father Leo took the situation in stride, patting heads and scratching ears as the two canines milled around their legs. Brent and Travis couldn't help smiling, especially since Demon, in particular, presented himself for tribute and let them scratch his ears. Brent felt a little awkward knowing Donny was also human, and offered a pat on the head in greeting.

"All right, all right, let's go inside." Mark shooed the two inside. He turned back to the others.

"Donny likes to shift when he comes to house sit. I guess that makes it more of a play date," he explained with a shrug. "They both seem to enjoy it, so I don't judge."

Donny wasn't in sight when they headed into Mark's living room. Mark offered drinks as Demon turned circles on his bed and settled down. Travis and Brent went for beer, Father Leo opted for a soda, and Mark tipped an ounce or two of whiskey into his cola before joining them.

"Grab a drink and come join us when you're ready," Mark yelled toward the back hallway, where Brent guessed Donny had gone. Minutes later, a lanky young man with floppy dark hair emerged, all human with sharp features like his malamute/husky side, with mismatched blue and gold eyes. He got a soda and took the chair closest to where Demon lay.

"What did you make of the service?" Father Leo looked to Brent and Travis in particular.

"Short and to the point," Brent replied. "Works for me. I'm not much for ceremony."

"Beats the heck out of a full funeral mass," Travis answered laconically.

Father Leo laughed. "It might be heresy, but I fully agree."

"Did those folks have particular ties to Al, or just the community showing up for one of their own?" Brent hadn't noted any striking resemblances to Al's photo, but he knew that in small towns, family links were common and convoluted.

"Bob, the guy who talked to you, was a cousin, if I remember right," Father Leo said. "Fred and Jimmy, two of the other older men, often hunted with Al. I think they blame themselves for not being with him when the rougarou got him, but that's how it goes."

"Either Janie or Andi might be a distant relative, but I'm not sure," Mark said. "They're damn fine hunters. Al always stood up for them if anyone got snarky, either about women hunting or them being a couple. Like I said, he was a good guy."

"Is the rougarou still out there?" Travis asked.

Brent understood the concern. Like lions or other normal predators, a carnivore that attacked a human lost its right to protection and was likely to kill again.

"No. The night we found Al, Bob called for a dragnet. We all went out moving in a grid. Got the son of a bitch. Nasty piece of work," Mark replied, and Brent thought he saw a flicker of grief in his eyes from his own loss to a similar monster.

"Good," Travis said quietly. Most of the time, hunters worked alone or with a partner, reserving such large, coordinated team efforts for particularly dangerous targets.

Brent sat back on the couch and sipped his cola. "If Al got killed by a rougarou, what makes you think someone is targeting the hunters? It's too bad he died, but it sounds like a normal hunt gone wrong. What's different?"

"We haven't had a rougarou in these parts for more than a decade," Mark said. "So where did one suddenly come from?"

Travis leaned forward with his elbows on his knees. "You think someone is herding or transporting monsters to up the stakes?"

Mark rolled his eyes. "I don't think they're being loaded into trailers and hauled here. But with the right magic, it seems to me they could be drawn to an area. Nudged, lured, whatever you want to call it."

Brent frowned, thinking. "Seems like a lot of work. Why? What's the goal?"

"It's not just here."

They all turned to look at Father Leo. "Our folks don't usually go as far north as Erie or too deep into the center of the state, but I'm hearing that they've had a spate of particularly vicious monsters and hunter deaths, too. Pretty much our corner of northwestern PA, down as far as your area."

Travis shifted in his seat, and Brent could guess his friend's thoughts. *That's a pretty close overlap with the local chapter of Sinistram.*

"Got any suspects?" Brent asked. "Pissed off a necromancer or a big coven? Riled up an ancient dark witch?"

"Not to our knowledge," Father Leo replied. "And that kind of retribution would likely be more personal, maybe take out a particular hunter or team. This...it's too targeted and frequent to be coincidence, but there's a short list of who benefits from not having hunters do their job, and I can't make the pieces fit."

"We just faced off with CHARON, so I don't think it's them. They think they're better than regular hunters, but they aren't usually on the monster's side," Brent mused.

"Don't take this the wrong way, but the people and places aren't usually on Sinistram's radar," Travis said. "They usually only concern themselves with situations they consider to be important—according to their criteria. Everything else is beneath them."

"If they set that aside for...reasons. Could they do it?" Father Leo asked.

Travis's gaze darted around the room, and Brent knew it was a sure sign he was searching his memories.

"Maybe. I guess so. Magically? I'm not sure what it would take to lure monsters from their regular territories over a distance. Too much sustained effort for one person, I'd think. And why would it matter if the hunters were killed in this area instead of back where the creatures were from originally? Dead is dead," Travis replied.

"How about a stealth third party?" Brent tossed out. "A wild card. Are there other people or groups who might have juiced up enough to do it? Secret supernatural groups seem to be a dime a dozen."

Mark sniffed. "You mean guys who are more hunter cosplay than the real thing? They watch some TV, cause problems at cemeteries, banish a couple of ghosts, and retreat to their clubhouse to drink and play poker. We've run into a few of them, but they're more likely to be the next casualties than the masterminds."

"Same with the witches," Father Leo said. "We have a few with real power, who, fortunately for us, are on our side. They do a very serious job of policing their own. If a dark practitioner tried to move into their territory, I suspect they'd deal with it and bury the body. One and done."

"Got any goth teenagers gone wrong? Folks who've seen too many movies and downloaded a grimoire from the Dark Web to summon Aleister Crowley and got Cthulhu instead?" Travis mused.

The Dark Web used ensorcelled encryption to safeguard its secrets and catered to those who worked with the supernatural and occult. What was accessible on the regular internet could be troublesome enough, but if someone had gotten past the protections, information on the Dark Web was far more dangerous.

"Not that we've heard, but anything's possible, I guess," Father Leo said. "We can check with our witchy friends. Janie and Andi are also pretty connected with the local covens. It won't hurt to ask."

"Whatever the reason, folks are nervous," Mark said. "Hunters are a superstitious bunch to start with, and a run of bad luck has them looking for omens in their tea leaves. If the fish aren't biting or there are more storms than usual or there's a weird moon like a little while ago, people whisper about 'connections.' I'll be glad when things settle down."

After that, the conversation shifted to football and the weather as they finished off the last of their drinks and the day caught up with them.

"I'm going to head out." Father Leo put his empty soda bottle in the recycling bin. "Good to see you again, Travis and Brent. Call anytime if I can help."

They said goodnight, and Mark went to a hallway closet, returning with an armful of sheets, blankets, and pillows.

"Someone gets the couch, and someone else gets the guest room. You can flip for it," Mark told them. "I get up pretty early to take Demon out, and then I get the coffee going. I have cereal, toast, and peanut butter. Not fancy, but it's free. Help yourselves. Don't leave without saying goodbye. I have a couple of ideas I need to sleep on. Don't worry about Donny. If he stays over, he stays in his wolf and sleeps with Demon. If you hear snoring, it's them, not me. Sleep tight."

With that, Mark headed down the hall and into his room. Brent looked at Travis. "Got a preference?"

"Go ahead and take the guest room. I'll take the couch," Travis volunteered. Brent suspected his friend offered because Brent's back was still sore after the cement factory fight.

"Thanks. You can get first dibs on the bathroom," Brent offered. He had packed a few essentials in his backpack, so it didn't take long for him to change into sleep pants and a T-shirt.

Snoring rumbled from the other room.

"Need earplugs?" Travis offered. "I always keep a few pairs handy."

Brent shook his head. "I'll be okay. Once you learn to sleep through a war zone, not much else bothers you." He dropped his voice. "The secret is to be so damn exhausted you can't stay awake even if they put the air raid siren next to your ear."

"I'll take your word on that," Travis replied. "Monasteries cornered the market on silence."

True to his word, Brent fell asleep quickly. When he woke the next morning, he heard Travis and Donny talking quietly in the kitchen. Demon had come out to wake him, plunking his huge head beside Brent's face and staring him into awareness with his warm brown eyes. The muffled sound of a shower told Brent where Mark had gone.

"Coffee's ready," Donny called. "There's a second bathroom at the end of the hall if you're desperate. Make yourself at home."

Brent ruffled Demon's ears and got a toothy grin in response, then he got up, rummaged in his backpack for fresh clothes, and went to change. When he walked into the kitchen, Travis shoved a cup of black coffee into his hands.

"Here. Caffeinate. You'll be less grumpy."

"Guilty as charged." He took the coffee, grabbed a toaster pastry, and ate it cold, eager to have the caffeine and sugar hit his system. After a second cup, he tuned into the conversation.

"I don't hear the insider gossip with the pack," Donny was saying. "Mark says I'm too wolfy for a lot of people and too people-y for a lot of wolves, and he's not wrong. I have my friends. Our pack is small and we don't cause trouble. We've had an understanding with the hunters around here for a long time. There's a lot to lose if someone breaks the truce and makes it look like our fault."

"Has that happened?" Travis gulped down his java and turned to get a refill.

"No, but with what you all talked about, it worries me. I trust Mark, but if hunters get trigger-happy because they think someone is attacking them, it could get bad."

Brent couldn't argue with his logic. "Has the pack noticed any suspicious magic? Any changes in the wild creatures?" He wanted to make it clear to Donny that he made a distinction between the animalistic monsters and those that had a human side, like werewolves, shifters, and vampires.

Some hunters, those who used hunting to act out their rage and trauma, considered everything supernatural to be a threat worthy of death. Brent, Travis, and other responsible hunters didn't associate with those folks.

"I've heard talk about sensing some strange energy," Donny replied. "Some of the older pack members have been patrolling, but I didn't get the feeling they'd found anything. Yet they were worried, that's unusual."

Anything that worries werewolves is worth taking seriously, Brent thought.

"You still up for heading to the mine after this?" Travis asked, changing the subject.

Brent tossed back his coffee and nodded. "Yeah. Figured we would."

"Mine monsters?" Donny sounded intrigued. Demon crunched kibble in his dish and slurped water, then curled up under the table.

"We're not completely sure what's going on," Travis admitted. "But it's another location where the ghosts from a long-ago tragedy are suddenly attacking people. Until we figure out how to stop the haunts from juicing up, we have to deal with the effects instead of the cause."

"What kind of mines?" Mark caught the end of the comment as he walked into the kitchen.

"Mostly coal mines. Old ones from the turn of the last century," Travis replied.

Mark grinned. "If you can spare the morning, I have some guys you need to meet. They know everything there is to know about those old mines, and they might have some insight into the ghosts and monsters, too."

Brent and Travis exchanged a glance. "Sure," Brent replied. "Although it's a kind of random specialty."

"Not to these guys," Mark replied. "And if we're lucky, we can also score a pretty damn good lunch to send you on your way."

"Are you going to fill us in?" Travis asked.

Mark's grin grew broader. "Nope. Don't worry. It's a good kind of surprise. Something to look forward to." He turned to Donny. "You okay here with Demon until I get back?"

"Sure. Take your time. We'll be here," Donny said.

Brent and Travis piled into Mark's pickup and headed out.

"Tell me about these mines," Mark said.

"The whole Pittsburgh area is like an ant hill of abandoned mine tunnels, mostly from the coal days back in the late 1800s," Travis said. "Some are mapped, most aren't. The companies merged, got bought, or went out of business, and lots of records got lost. It was dangerous work, and lots of men died."

"But there were some disasters that stood out, even with that," Brent jumped in. "The Darr Mine was the big one." He filled Mark in on the information Travis had shared just the day before. "The Mammoth Mine was also really bad, and the Naomi Mine disaster wasn't as large a death toll, but it's in the same local area."

"People still tell stories about the explosions, the men who died, how the companies covered up their safety failures," Travis added. "And there have been legend trippers who went looking for the mine openings, although they've been relatively well sealed for decades. But lately, the stories changed.

"People started hearing screams from where the old mines were, and seeing ghosts in the woods and along the roads nearby, men in old-time clothing like they're hitching a ride home," Travis went on. "Plus reports of loud knocking sounds coming from inside the mines."

"Odd, given how long ago the disasters happened and that there wasn't a big anniversary of the incident or someone trying to redevelop either the mines or the land around them," Brent added.

"But in the last month, there've been deaths," Brent continued. "That's a new twist. Local deer hunters, hikers, and urban explorers were all found dead near the mine sites, and they all died from firedamp."

Mark frowned. "I don't know what that is."

"Methane," Brent said. "It occurs naturally in coal mines, and one danger is that it's explosive. But if people breathe it in, they asphyxiate. And the recent deaths were all people who had methane in their lungs, but hadn't broken the sealed openings to the mine entrances."

"Does methane like that show up anywhere else?" Mark asked.

"Tunnels and marshes in a coal-heavy area, but that's much less often than in mines," Travis replied. "And there weren't any open tunnels or nearby marshes where the dead men were found."

"What did the cops say?" Mark took a gulp of his coffee from his travel mug.

"Not much," Travis replied. "They chalked it up to people fooling around with dangerous inhalants, although I've never heard of anyone sniffing methane for a high. One of the reports blamed local pollution. Combined with the screams and the ghost sightings, it seems more likely that we've got some dormant hauntings that suddenly turned ugly. But it's hard to shut down a haunt when you don't know what's feeding it energy."

Mark didn't drive far before he pulled into the dirt driveway of a fairground. "We're here," he proclaimed as they drove under a banner that read, "Old Timers' Steam and Gas Engine Show."

"An engine show?" Travis sounded perplexed.

They hadn't even paid their entrance fee yet, and Brent could hear the loud chugging noises and smell the smoke that hung like a cloud over the property. As they drove toward the parking area, he saw signs pointing toward a frontier village, as well as posters advertising food, a swap meet, craft and engine demonstrations, and live music.

"These engines date from the same time as your mine disasters," Mark told them as they got out of the truck and walked toward the main attraction, rows upon rows of huge old machines. Most of the engines were the size of modern cars or larger. Made of solid steel and cast iron, they were impressive workhorses with flywheels as tall as Travis.

Mixed among the gigantic engines were vintage tractors and farm equipment as well as horse-drawn wagons. A sign gave times for upcoming horse-powered tractor pulls. Older men in trucker caps and bib overalls talked to visitors, animatedly explaining the equipment.

"Those old coal mines used engines like these for all kinds of tasks." Mark led them into the main exhibit area, which had already drawn a crowd despite the early hour. "And the guys who collect this stuff are true historians. They know everything there is to know about the type of engine they collect, but also about where particular pieces came from and how they were used."

Brent looked around, taking in the sights. He vaguely remembered seeing ads for similar events, but hadn't given them much thought. From the fascinated expressions of the visitors and the clear enthusiasm of the docents, he realized they were entering a well-established "fandom" that was entirely new territory.

"Do you know these folks?" Travis asked. They walked past the entrance to the food area, where smokers and grills were already preparing for the lunch crowd. Brent took a deep breath and couldn't hide the way his stomach rumbled.

Mark nodded. "We're all mechanics, just different types of motors. The connections come in handy. Some of these guys make parts because there's nothing on the market for pieces this old. I don't work on cars that are technically antiques, but it's surprisingly difficult to find replacement parts for anything that's ten years or older."

He led Travis and Brent toward a hulking engine that was easily the size of a compact car, with a cylindrical body, a powerful piston arm, and a wide flywheel.

"Hey Ted!" Mark shouted above the noise of the engines. "Need to introduce you to some friends." He made the introductions and everyone shook hands.

"Travis and Brent came up from Pittsburgh, and they're interested in some of the big mine disasters around there, like the Darr Mine," Mark said.

Ted's eyebrows rose. "Wow, that's going back a while. What got you looking at that?"

"Amateur historians," Travis replied, which was mostly true. "The Mammoth Mine and Naomi Mine also came up in the research."

Ted shook his head. "Tragedies, all of them, and close together by location and time too. That kind of thing happened a lot back then."

"I told them that you and your friends probably knew everything about those mines, at least when it came to the engines that kept them running," Mark flattered.

Ted grinned. "Well, I wouldn't say *everything*, but maybe a good bit. Little different focus, more on how they operated than on the disasters."

"Did they use engines like that one?" Travis nodded toward the chugging machine close enough that they had to raise their voices to be heard.

"Oh, yeah. This is an Otto, a goddamn workhorse that was used in mines, saw mills, and all kinds of factories. As you can see, this version of the engine was intended to be stationary." Ted warmed to the topic. "Mr. Otto wasn't interested in other uses, but two people who worked for him—named Daimler and Maybach—adapted it for automobiles. The company Otto founded is still in business, one of the largest engine-makers."

Brent recognized the names from the cars and companies that were their namesakes. "It's hard to believe that something so big inspired the sort of engines we're still using."

"See, that's part of what gets people hooked on this stuff," Ted said. "Plus, they sound really cool when they run." Boyish glee glinted in his eyes. "Otto engines are some of the quietest of the bunch."

"Going back to the mines, what did the engines do?" Travis brought the conversation back on topic.

"For coal mines, engines like this one ran the pumps that brought water out of the mines," Ted said. "Some of them could even use the dangerous methane as fuel."

"They were built to last," he went on. "You see that one over there?" He pointed to a similar engine that looked very hard-used. "It survived the Darr Mine explosion because it was up near the mine mouth, but you can see that it got beat up pretty good from flying rock. Not everyone is happy I brought it—some folks say it's haunted."

"Oh really?" Travis exchanged a glance with Brent.

Ted chuckled. "If you believe in that sort of thing. I bought it off a guy whose great-grandfather handled the sell-off of whatever assets were left when the mine shut down. Funny thing is that I've been over every inch of it and there's nothing wrong with it, but it won't run."

He leaned forward. "But sometimes at night, I'll be in the house and I hear the engine running. I know it isn't, and I go out to check, and it's quiet and cold. Usually happens in December, right around the time of the disaster. Like it remembers."

"Do you hear a lot of stories about the mines being haunted?" Travis managed to sound off-handed.

"Sure, plenty of them," Ted replied. "It was a dangerous way to make a living, and there were a whole lot of ways to die. The history books remember the big disasters like the explosions and the cave-ins, but the truth is that dozens of men died every week in those big mines. Some of their spirits moved on and some didn't."

"In the stories you've heard, did any of those hauntings turn dangerous?" Brent asked. "There are some tales going around lately that sound like the ghosts might have decided to get revenge."

"After all this time? Wow, that's interesting, although I'm not surprised. The Darr engine probably could have been fixed up to work again, but it's what folks call a 'hoodoo engine.' Any locomotive or engine like this that was involved in a tragedy or just never ran quite right got a reputation for being unlucky, like a hoodoo curse," Ted told them.

"You don't seem worried," Brent observed.

Ted shrugged. "I'm not very superstitious, but I take precautions. Never tried to start the Darr engine, never will. Haul it all by itself, on an iron bed, blessed by a priest with holy water. I store it in its own corner, not near anything that could catch fire or fall down, and there's a ring of rock salt around it, just in case."

"Why bother? Travis asked. "Why take a chance, in case the superstition is true?"

Ted sighed. "I get asked that. Closest thing I can tell you is that those miners deserve to be remembered, and keeping the engine gives me a reason to tell their story. Their bosses cut corners, and hundreds of men died. I don't think we've learned the lesson yet."

Brent and Travis thanked Ted and walked through the display to the Darr engine. Both men kept their distance from the machine, staying several feet away.

"Do you see anything?" Mark asked.

Travis nodded. "There's a swirl of spirits around the engine. They don't seem angry or dangerous, but they're staying close to the Otto, so they're not just ghosts from the park." He paused. "There's one in particular, a man in his young teens, who seems particularly connected."

Travis closed his eyes and concentrated. "Sadness. Loss. Despair." He opened them to look at the engine. "It belongs in a memorial. I understand Ted's reasons for keeping it, but I certainly wouldn't want that energy near me all the time."

"Look: salt." Brent pointed to where a faint ring of white could be seen through the park's crabgrass.

Travis looked out over the rest of the display. Brent heard people talking, children laughing, and live music from the direction of the food court. Either they weren't picking up on the psychic residue, or it didn't bother them.

They moved on, following Mark to stroll around the grounds. "I don't know if other people have engines from different disasters, but I wouldn't doubt it. Although they might not be as willing to talk about it," Mark told them. "Thought you ought to hear his story for yourselves."

"Yeah, thank you. Not sure what to make of it, but it's another piece to the puzzle," Brent replied. "And just in general, this show is pretty cool."

"I know, right?" Mark grinned. "Once we make the rounds, we'll get you fed and send you on your way. The food is awesome."

The frontier village was a set of storefronts made to look like an Old West town where craftspeople sold everything from handmade soap to leatherwork and more. Women spun yarn on spinning wheels while talking to customers, who reminisced about the past.

Outside, a fiddler struck up a lively tune near where people carried plates of grilled meat and all the fixings to picnic tables.

They dug into their food, leaving conversation for later. When they cleared their trays and headed back toward the parking area, Brent bumped Travis's arm.

"Penny for your thoughts."

Travis chuckled. "You'll get to hear them all the way back to Pittsburgh for free. But at the moment, other than thinking lunch was really good, I was considering how people take for granted things from the mine could be haunted. It's not a new idea."

"Given the death toll, the places should be lousy with spirits," Brent replied. "My question is, why aren't they?"

"Because the mines and mills and factories employed their own witches."

They both turned to look at Mark, who shrugged. "I heard about it from my dad and grandpa, but other people heard the stories, too," he said. "I guess it was cheaper to hire a witch to dispel the ghosts than it was to fix whatever safety problems kept killing people."

"That makes sense...in a sick sort of way," Brent admitted.

"And now, after all this time, the old protections are faltering," Travis said. "If the rumors are right and someone or some group is causing trouble, or there's a bad moon rising, breaking what's left of those spells might have helped."

"More dangerous for civilians, but also for the hunters," Mark agreed.

They drove back to Mark's place. Travis and Brent put their backpacks in Travis's car. "Thanks for everything, Mark. Let us know if you hear anything else," Brent said.

"Still going to the Darr Mine today?" Mark asked.

Brent looked to Travis, who nodded. "It'll be early afternoon by the time we get there. Might be nice not to be tripping over tree roots in the dark for once," he replied.

"You need me to follow you down and lend a hand?" Mark asked.

Travis shook his head. "Thanks, but I think we've got it. Be sure to tell Donny and Father Leo we said goodbye."

"Of course, if we get thrown around too much, we might need to call you about those two other mines with ghost problems," Brent added.

"You know where to find me," Mark told them. "Unless something dire happens, I'm spending the next couple of days in the garage, catching up on some repairs and bodywork."

Travis and Brent waved as they pulled out of his driveway and headed to the mine. They had everything necessary in the trunk, including shotguns, rock salt, holy water, and a grenade launcher, just in case.

They rode with just the music from the radio for the first while. Brent was thinking about everything they had seen and heard, trying to fit the new information with what they previously knew, looking for the all-important holes in what they were missing.

"You still think we're dealing with a tommyknocker?" Brent asked after they had driven for a while.

Travis nodded. "Mine lore is big on trolls, gnomes, and those kinds of creatures," he replied. "Tommyknockers and *coblyns* show up in the lore from Cornwall, and the earliest miners at Darr would have been from Cornwall and Wales before the Poles and Slovaks came. For most of them, the remedy was the same: a binding spell and iron chains."

"Like the kind we usually keep on hand?" More than one type of creature required sturdy restraints if Brent and Travis weren't able to deal with them right away. A locked box in the trunk held weapons and specialized gear. A blacksmith not far from Pittsburgh understood the supernatural and supplied them with the kind of equipment they couldn't find at the hardware store.

"Yeah. I found sigils that are supposed to drain power from mountain creatures, which would include tommyknockers," Travis replied. "I carved them into the set of cuffs we have in the back."

"The challenge is going to be putting them on," Brent pointed out. "I don't imagine it'll stand still if you ask nicely."

"Probably not. That's where you come in. Distract it. Weaken him with salt, iron, and silver shot. Give me an opening to slap the cuffs on him."

Brent gave him a side-eye look. "Sure. You make it sound easy."

"Never promised that," Travis said. "But the lore didn't give me other options. They can be bound, but they can't be killed."

"If that's the case, what are the odds that whatever or whoever is killing hunters broke the binding early?" Brent asked. "The timing could be a coincidence...but it's suspicious."

"Agree. And I don't know," Travis admitted. "There's no way to know how long ago someone bound the Darr creature, or how long the binding was supposed to last. It might have worn off...or someone could have taken advantage of an old, weakened spell to end it early. I can't prove it, but I suspect our mysterious someone set the tommy-knocker loose early."

"Yeah, I'm thinking the same thing."

They rode in silence for a while before Travis spoke up again. "Do you think the type of mine witches changed over the years? Because where the miners came from shifted over time. At first, way back, it was mostly from Wales and Cornwall. Later on, Germany, Hungary, and Poland."

"Depends on what the witch was meant to do." Brent wasn't surprised that they had apparently been thinking along the same lines. "If it was to control any creature or spirit that was part of the mine itself, that wouldn't matter. But if it was to bind the ghosts of the miners, then maybe magic from their home country worked better."

"We already put out feelers with our witch friends for help," Travis said. "Guess this is one more for the list, looking for people with knowledge about those magical traditions. Still plenty of people who hail from those places in Pittsburgh. I'm hoping it won't be too hard to find some."

They changed clothes at a rest stop, exchanging their more presentable jeans and shirts for harder-used versions and grabbing small protective bags of salt from the trunk to tuck into pockets. Travis and Brent always wore silver protective amulets, but they added bracelets just in case.

Brent glanced at his watch and the position of the sun. "Not far from here. Might be done in time for supper."

"Don't jinx us," Travis replied, only partly in jest.

Close to the turnoff, a historical marker commemorated the disaster, a raised granite square with the name and date of the event. Brent figured it was better than nothing, but it seemed insufficient for a tragedy that claimed so many lives. He knew that a Hungarian civic organization had donated a tombstone to mark the common grave at a nearby cemetery where the bodies had been interred.

The road to the old mine entrance showed up on antique maps, but just looked like an unmarked driveway on the electronic version. Brent had expected chain-link fences and warning signs, but nothing kept them from pulling the car far enough onto the approach to not be visible.

They loaded up on weapons and other equipment and hiked in. The forest had reclaimed the land, but a close look revealed the remnants of development.

"There's the mouth of the mine." Travis pointed to a rocky overhang in a hillside that had filled with debris and largely overgrown with roots.

"Glad we don't have to go inside," Brent said with a shiver.

"Me, too." Travis nodded to a cracked rectangular slab of old concrete near the mine mouth. It looked like something had been ripped free despite secure fasteners.

"Want to bet that's where Ted's engine sat? One of the accounts said that a miner was found pinned beneath a ten-ton engine that had been thrown from its moorings," Travis said.

"Jesus," Brent breathed. "Guess that explains the man's ghost you saw with the Otto at the show." He concentrated. "There are a lot of spirits nearby. They're watching us. Maybe they're used to hikers."

"Except something killed three visitors," Travis pulled what he needed from his bag to handle the magical part of the banishment. Brent readied weapons in case the attacks involved something more corporeal.

"You ready?" Travis asked when he had everything in place.

"As much as I'm ever going to be," Brent replied.

They had already agreed to focus on whatever creature resided in the mine, not banishing ghosts unless the spirits proved dangerous.

"The ghosts don't want us here, but I think they're trying to protect us," Travis shouted as the wind grew stronger, stirring the branches overhead and raising dust and dead leaves.

"Creature of the mine! You have caused enough harm. Leave this place and do not return." Travis repeated the invocation in Latin and then again in Polish, like Mark had taught him.

The temperature dropped, and now the wind carried the echoes of the doomed miners' shrieks and screams.

"Show yourself and depart. Trouble the living no more," Travis commanded. He drew a banishment sigil in the ground with an iron bar.

Brent's Glock had silver bullets, and the shotgun slung over his shoulder held rock salt rounds. Silver and iron knives hung at his belt, and a rowan wood staff leaned against a tree within reach.

Loud thumps came from inside the old mine entrance. The ghosts had enough energy to appear like a gray cloud, a fury of moans and screams, interposing their whirlwind between the two hunters and the mine.

More thumps, louder now and closer. Whatever was inside had reacted to Travis's incantation, heading toward them whether it intended to fight or depart.

The ghosts exploded from the mouth of the mine with gusts of wind that nearly knocked Travis and Brent off their feet. Whether the creature had contributed to the mine disaster or merely come later like a scavenger, the spirits clearly saw it as the enemy.

One second, the mine entrance looked undisturbed, and the next, a monster stood facing them, although the gateway remained sealed.

"Holy shit!" Brent shouted above the wind.

The short, squat creature only stood as high as Brent's shoulders. Wrinkled, leathery skin covered its powerfully built body, except for a shock of tangled brown hair on its head. Its arms and legs were disproportionately long, and its hands and feet ended in wicked talons. Broken manacles dangled from the creature's wrists and ankles. "That's a tommyknocker, all right," Travis said with a grim set to his jaw. "They're a nasty piece of work."

The tommyknocker's eyes squinted as if unused to the light. A pointed nose and sharp cheekbones resembled drawings Brent had seen of gremlins, right down to the mouthful of vicious teeth.

The creature rushed at Brent, covering the distance faster than he expected. It swiped at him, and a talon ripped down his shirt, raising a trail of blood as it caught the skin beneath.

Brent shot at the monster, trying to buy time for Travis to finish his spell. The tommyknocker's speed made it hard to hit, and the bullets that struck its tough skin didn't slow it down.

The creature barreled into Brent, knocking him backward into a rusted section of old fence. Brent reached above his head, grabbed hold of the metal, and drew up both feet, kicking the mine monster in the chest with his full strength.

It staggered back, and Brent fired point-blank as it came at him again.

Brent knew magic couldn't be rushed, but he feared that he might not survive long enough to keep Travis safe until the mine could be sealed and the creature banished.

Black ichor seeped from the bullet wounds, proving Brent's shots had hurt it, but not enough to stop the attack. Ghosts swept in like a gray tide, trying to slow the creature down and keep him from reaching Brent. It swiped at the spirits with its long talons, and to

Brent's astonishment, the monster's claws shredded the ghosts, who shrieked and vanished.

Out of bullets, Brent grabbed a length of steel pipe off the ground and swung two-handed, landing a bone-jarring blow to the tommyknocker's head. It bared its jagged teeth and screamed in fury, throwing itself at Brent. The ghosts rushed between Brent and the creature, creating a whirlwind to slow its attack. Travis switched to a new incantation, one Brent recognized as a defensive spell. The monster slowed, then stopped as if trapped by an invisible force.

Brent switched to his shotgun and fired at the tommyknocker's head and chest. The salt rounds affected the creature even more than the silver, and it stopped struggling.

"Cover me!" Travis rushed in with the new cuffs and chains, forged of iron. "I'm going to bind it."

"By the power of iron and silver, I send you back into the deep places. Remain there, and do not trouble the living again." Travis slammed the bindings closed on the tommyknocker's wrists and ankles.

The monster's image wavered, then blinked out. Appeased, the ghosts quieted, still powerful enough to make themselves seen even to those without special abilities. That meant Brent saw faces and forms in the cloud around them, haggard men and boys who died before their time.

"Thank you," Brent told the ghosts. "Thank you for protecting me, and for trying to protect the people the creature killed. That should keep him bound for a long time. Go in peace and take your rest."

The ghostly images grew fainter and then vanished on the wind. Brent blew out a breath and turned to Travis.

"Did you see that?"

Travis nodded. "Yep. You, okay?"

"I want to sleep for a week, but it could have been worse." Brent thought of the tommyknocker's sharp claws and shuddered.

"How long do you think that will hold him? Another century?"

Brent looked for shell casings and other evidence, satisfied when he was certain they had left nothing behind but salt.

"With luck. Maybe we can find a heritage group to preserve the knowledge of what we did so the binding can be renewed before it completely runs out," Travis said as they packed out.

"You think that's what we'll find at Mammoth Mine, too? It's had the same sort of attacks."

"Maybe, but the devil's in the details. I need to look deeper into how the mountain monsters differ. Don't want to find out that for the one particular type we come up against, the fix we've been using doesn't work," Travis replied.

"That would be...awkward."

"To say the least."

Brent knew they had been lucky today. Neither of them had been badly injured, which was a rarity. They couldn't count on that, even when going up against a similar creature. A bit of bad luck could change everything in a matter of seconds.

Travis gave him a worried once-over. "You're hurt. We need Matthew to clean those cuts so they don't get infected."

"Dinner before doctor," Brent said. "We can eat in the car while we drive. I look like I lost a fight with a rabid bobcat."

They grabbed burgers from a drive-through and stopped at St. Dismas long enough for Matthew to treat Brent's wounds. It was dark by the time Travis pulled up to the curb in front of Brent's house.

"Let me follow up on those witch contacts, and I'll let you know what I find," Travis told him as Brent grabbed his backpack.

"Sounds good to me. I could use a couple of days in the office, but I'll be ready to go whenever you are." Brent tapped the roof of the car in parting and headed inside as Travis drove away.

He flicked the lights on and dropped his backpack next to the couch, then went to the kitchen and pulled a beer from the fridge. Brent grabbed the remote and turned on a football game just for background noise.

Now that the fight had a chance to sink in, Brent braced himself for the aftereffects. The crash from a life-or-death conflict was a wicked backlash from the heightened energy and senses a surge of adrenaline provided. Despite being physically exhausted, he knew that even with a couple of beers, he would need several hours to relax enough to even try to sleep.

A flicker of movement made him look up. The ghost of his brother, Danny, sat cross-legged on the floor between Brent and the television.

Danny and Brent had always been exceptionally close as twins. Then Danny died, and while Brent often sensed his brother's presence, he couldn't see or hear him without a medium's help. But after Brent's fight with a demon and Danny's sacrifice and return, something changed, and Brent had been able to see Danny's ghost more often, although he still couldn't summon him or hear him without assistance.

"We did good tonight," Brent told him, hoping Danny could hear him even if he couldn't hear his ghostly brother's response. "Got rid of a real, honest-to-goodness mine monster. You'd have loved it."

Danny rolled his eyes, but his smile tempered the dismissal. Brent didn't want him anywhere near their battles because he knew that ghosts could be damaged and banished even though they were dead. And while Brent hoped Danny would eventually find rest, he couldn't deny that his occasional presence soothed some of the loss and loneliness.

"Got to admit, I'm worried." Talking to his brother's ghost was easier sometimes than confessing his uneasiness to Travis. "Something's juicing up the monsters and going after hunters, and I'm afraid we don't know the full story. I think there's more to it, a bigger bad, and we'd better figure it out fast or I'll be seeing you sooner rather than later."

Danny's easy-going grin shifted to a stern frown. Brent didn't need words to know his brother worried about the dangers of hunting and wanted Brent to be safe.

"Yeah, yeah. I'm not in a hurry, although I do miss having you around. I just can't shake the feeling that there's an enemy out there we've underestimated or aren't seeing, and it's going to bite us on the ass if we don't catch on quick."

Danny cocked his head questioningly. Brent had gotten good at guessing his intentions.

"I don't know if you can help. Please don't risk being hurt or sent away."

Danny looked annoyed, and Brent had to chuckle at the familiar expression. "Maybe just keep your ears open around the other ghosts? I don't know how much gossip there is in the afterlife, but if you hear something, let me know. Or better yet, you can always go to Travis."

Danny grinned and nodded. He put his hand over his heart and then waved goodbye as he faded out.

While being able to interact with Danny's ghost was a blessing, nothing made up for his absence.

"Love you too, idiot," Brent grumbled before he tossed off the rest of his beer and headed for bed, resigned to yet another sleepless night.

CHAPTER THREE

"WHY ARE YOU HERE?" The old priest didn't try to hide the disdain in his voice.

"Because someone a lot closer to the Pope than you gave me permission," Travis replied.

"Your apostasy makes the Holy Father weep."

"And you know that, how?" Travis shouldered past the priest and entered the Sinistram library. Travis avoided the library except when he had no choice but to find what he needed. It was true that he had been granted special dispensation to retain access to the books even after leaving the Sinistram and the priesthood. Travis knew it wasn't a kindness. Those at the top hoped it would be an inducement to get him to return.

That meant they didn't fathom the depths of his hatred for the organization and its methods.

"You need to be escorted," the priest said. He was one of the Keepers, the guardians of the library and its mysteries. The Keepers served the Sinistram with magic and knowledge, fighting battles on an arcane level that were no less deadly than those waged in person.

"So, escort. I'm not stopping you."

Travis knew his way around the arcane repository, filled with grimoires, spell books, and the notebooks of generations of mage-priests. Much of the information stored here was forbidden; all of it was dangerous, especially its extensive collection on demonology.

The library occupied a warren of tunnels deep beneath the Duquesne University Seminary Library. Rumor had it that the tunnels and arcane library predated the university and were the reason for its fortified position on a cliffside overlooking the river.

Floor-to-ceiling shelves were filled with books, scrolls, boxes, and manuscripts. The bare electric bulbs overhead struggled against the shadows. Its perpetual chill made Travis shiver.

Learning his way around had taken time and stubbornness, but Travis had persisted despite the library Keepers' over-protectiveness. That served him well when, like today, he had a quest that he preferred not to explain.

He easily navigated to the section on creatures. In the Sinistram's eyes, everything that wasn't human was a monster. Travis had gained a more nuanced perspective, based on what someone or something did, not what they were.

The organization made an exception for magic and mediumship because the talents were useful, but preferred to rely on sharply honed fighting and weapons skills to accomplish their objectives.

The Sinistram remained the secretive "left hand of the Holy Father," a supernatural strike force that carried out dangerous missions against paranormal threats. They were the kind of guys who shriveled the nuts off the biggest badass in the room and considered themselves to be above both mortal and canonical law, although neither set of authorities fully agreed.

If the Knights Templar were the Marines of the Vatican and the Occulatum was its FBI, Sinistram was the Church's Black Ops. Its pitiless ascetic culture and the ways in which it was willing to bend the power and morality of the church took a toll on its operatives, many of whom died young. Those who did not were fully given over to the Sinistram's ways.

Travis found the portion of the stacks he wanted, with his Keeper in tow. He scanned down the spines of the old books for the section on mountain dwellers, but something farther down the shelf caught his attention.

An entire section had been removed, hundreds of books spanning most of a millennium, written in many languages and containing lore from dozens of cultures.

Travis had studied those books many times and knew their value both as history and research tools. Finding that they had all been removed was disturbing.

"Why are the vampire books missing?" Travis asked.

His escort shrugged. "How should I know? It's a big library, and there are many with access. I assume someone needed them."

Travis caught the falsehood in the man's voice suggesting he knew more than he chose to say. He didn't call the man on his omission, but made a mental note, wondering who had wanted those particular books and why. Nothing from the library went missing or was misplaced. Those who worked in the library tended it with fierce devotion, making it their life's calling. They knew the location of every book, and if any were borrowed or removed for repair, it was known and recorded, tracked by administrative magic.

"I need a table and time to study." Travis brought his own notepad, knowing that he was not permitted to remove any of the books.

"Nothing has changed since your last visit. You know where to find what you need. I will quietly keep you company," the priest replied.

Travis moved through the familiar aisles, keeping an eye out for other groups of books that might have been removed. The werewolf section was still in place, as were categories for other groups of beings with supernatural abilities, except for the shelves for necromancy, where individual books appeared to be missing but not the entire collection. He tucked that away to consider later, when he could talk with Brent and Father Pavel, his friend and confessor.

Travis found a table and settled in, ignoring the priest who stood silently watching him, hands clasped, expression unreadable. Linen archival gloves protected the old pages from oil and sweat, but in Travis's case, also provided a thin barrier between him and the visions the old books might spark. He combed through the antique volumes, jotting notes to extend the knowledge he had already gained about the mine monsters.

Some of the tomes had nothing new, but others provided alternatives that his original sources did not mention.

Given the age of the library and its holdings, it didn't surprise Travis when he found a mention of the Mammoth Mine.

"Bingo," he murmured. "It's not a tommyknocker at the Mammoth Mine. They've got a bona fide evil gnome."

Travis dug into the information, not surprised to find contradictions since the records were old and spanned many traditions.

"They consider the mountains to belong to them, and prefer to inhabit natural caves and tunnels," he read aloud, fighting off drowsiness. "Some gnomes have made peace with sharing their mountain with miners, while others resent the intrusion and harass the miners with varying acts of sabotage."

Travis jotted down notes to share with Brent as they planned their strategy. While the depictions of gnomes from old woodcuts weren't as bloodthirsty as the tommyknockers, their expressions promised mayhem and danger.

Mark Wojcik had mentioned mine witches. On a sudden impulse, Travis decided to see if the Sinistram took note of such a lowly vocation. Mine witches were likely to be local healers with enough magic to do blessings and protection spells that held a modicum of power.

Maybe even the parish priest, if the padre had some magic on the side.

While the Sinistram involved itself in potentially world-ending events, the library's remarkably broad scope contained information on all kinds of magic, preserved in the safety of the archive. Travis hoped some long-ago librarian had found the topic worthy and stashed texts on the subject.

He grinned when he found three books that looked likely, tucked away with Latin tomes on subterranean magic.

Travis scanned the pages, taking notes. The first book traced the history of witches who protected wells, mines, tunnels, and other deep places. While he found it fascinating for the perspective, the book provided few specifics on what, exactly, the witches did or how they did it.

He sighed and started into the second book. It looked more promising, since the first pages acknowledged that the writer was a parish priest who infused his blessings and wards with magic beyond what the Eucharist provided.

The priest acknowledged that even magic couldn't completely protect against rock slides, collapses, bad air, or explosions. Yet he remained firmly convinced that the toll of deaths and injuries would be higher without the magic and that they were effective against all but the worst catastrophes.

He made note of the litanies and rituals that were cited, but frowned as once more, the book failed to address the presence of actual monsters among the dangers faced by those who toiled underground.

Finally, in the third book, he found what he'd been looking for. The author was a parish priest who documented life in a mining community in the late 1800s, around the time of the Darr disaster.

The priest clearly recognized the dangers faced by his parishioners and the fear that gripped their loved ones every day. He slipped in enough veiled digs to make it clear he faulted the mine owners for cutting corners that increased the risks.

When Father Illich learned that the town's mine witch was too elderly to continue his work, the priest went to the witch and asked to learn the rituals. Travis applauded the man for his open-mindedness and could have cheered out loud when the author wrote down the specific incantations, mantras, spells, and wards.

The next several pages detailed the different mine monsters he had encountered, what worked against them, and what had not. Tommyknockers were mentioned, as well as trolls, gnomes, and *coblyns*, among others.

"Can you see if there are more manuscripts by this author?" he asked the Keeper. "If there's something unbound, it wouldn't be with the books."

The priest looked unhappy to be bothered, but disappeared into the stacks long enough for Travis to use his phone to photograph the key pages. The Keepers prohibited phones or cameras, more a nod to tradition than for any real reason related to magic.

He took plenty of notes, careful to have his phone out of sight by the time the Keeper returned.

"No, sorry."

"Thanks for checking."

Travis turned the page and found a faded newspaper clipping about the Mammoth Mine disaster. The priest's handwriting on the bottom of the clip read, "gnome."

His fingers brushed the old article, and suddenly the library seemed to disappear, leaving him in the dank cold of the mine.

Travis's mind knew that visions weren't real, but his body reacted to the threat anyhow. *The air smelled of wet rock, oil lamps, and the exhaust fumes of the huge engine at the mine mouth. In the echo chamber of the tight tunnel, the engine's cycle sounded like a mechanical heartbeat, reverberating from the stone walls.*

Sweaty, dirt-streaked men crowded into the narrow entrance, and Travis could see the fear in their eyes they tried to hide. These men—some of them only boys—knew that the odds were against them returning home, and faced that fear every day. Most of them looked overtired and underfed, scraping out a living in this new land that barely kept them and their families alive.

Voices buzzed around him, speaking in Polish, Croatian, Hungarian, and heavily accented English. Many had been miners in their home countries before they came to Pennsylvania, hoping for a fresh start. They knew the dangers and gambled that, at least for today, luck would be with them.

At the mouth of the mine, silhouetted against the light, Travis glimpsed a man whose arms were lifted in benediction. The thunder of the engine kept him from hearing most of the words, but he felt the tingle of magic as the spell swept over and past the men, deep into the tunnel where the monsters lurked.

When the miners moved, they swept Travis along with them, into claustrophobic tunnels that opened into cavernous rooms where the coal was chipped from the rock by pickaxes and sledgehammers. Some of the men carried open flame lanterns, and other lamps hung from hooks high in the rock pillars.

A few men had gone deeper into the tunnel and returned. Travis saw them argue with the overseer. He couldn't pick up much, just "bad air." Their report didn't sway the man, who sent them back to their task. Murmurs and whispers circulated among the other men even as they stuck with their work.

Travis tried to draw a deep breath and found it difficult, as if his lungs were already full of something they couldn't dispel. He coughed and gagged, trying to clear his throat. Smoke mingled with the tang of methane and fine rock grit that Travis could taste in his mouth.

Then he saw it, a misshapen shadow against the lamplight, lurching toward them. Seconds later, an explosion rang out behind the creature, and a ball of flames raced around and past him.

Men screamed and tried to run. Travis remained frozen, an unlucky observer of the tragedy. The fire that engulfed the miners didn't affect the creature. Its red eyes gleamed, and just before Travis's vision faded, he saw the monster's lips pull back in a saw-toothed smile.

Travis woke gasping for breath, face down on the table. His whole body shook, and he swore he could still feel the fire and taste the methane.

I saw it. I saw the disaster and the monster.

"Your time is up."

Travis had almost forgotten the Keeper had stayed with him, and he managed not to startle at the interruption. Whatever the priest made of Travis's vision, it had not moved him to offer help.

"Because it's clearly so busy in here?" Travis snarked, still trying to regain his presence of mind. He shut the priest's memoir, careful not to touch the old clipping again.

The keeper was not amused. "The magic and spirits in these books make them dangerous. Contact must be limited to avoid possession or worse."

Travis always doubted the dire predictions the Keepers gave about restricting time in the library with the magical tomes. Although his skepticism suspected that the library minders didn't want to be responsible for their visitors for longer periods of time, he knew that many in the Sinistram did not question the idea that the library and its contents were dangerous, to be avoided if possible, and if not, consumed in as small amounts as possible.

"I think I've gotten what I need." Travis hid his annoyance. He carefully packed away his notebook and knew the Keeper would insist on reshelving the books he had used.

The Keeper followed him out of the stacks and the restricted area, a silent shadow. At the doorway, he paused.

"Don't return until the period of cleansing is completed," he warned. "For the good of your soul."

"I'll remember that." Travis brushed off the priest's concern.

"Mind your manners," the Keeper snapped. "You're merely a guest here."

So many things ran through Travis's mind to say in reply, but he swallowed them down. Picking a fight with someone who could turn a person into a frog—even temporarily—wasn't worth the hassle.

"Then I thank you for your warm welcome." Travis met the Keeper's gaze without flinching. "And I'm sure I'll be back as soon as I can."

The heavy iron door clanged shut behind Travis, and he paused to take a deep breath, feeling as if a weight had been lifted from his chest.

He didn't take the library's magic lightly. As a medium, he knew the archive had layers of protection, both from spells and from the cadre of ghostly priests who never left their posts even after their lives were over. They flitted just at the edge of his sight, usually ignoring him, but on occasion dropping or pulling out a book that was exactly what Travis needed.

No matter how much he hated returning to the Sinistram stronghold or how it would spark nightmares for days afterwards, he would not compromise a hunt for his personal comfort. He accepted the library's effect on him as a form of penance for the gray areas fighting monsters often required.

The Crown Vic was where he left it, untouched despite the dodgy area, protected by subtle distraction spells.

Danger. Run. The warning came from the ghost of a boy with a world-weary look in his eyes.

A bullet zinged by Travis, barely missing his shoulder. Clearly the spell didn't extend to distracting attackers from Travis as well as the car. Three men stepped out of the shadows, clearly lying in wait for him to return.

Travis dropped and crouched behind the Crown Vic, pulling his gun. He popped up, returning fire. That kept the men at bay for now, but he was likely to run out of ammo before they did, and a shootout in this area was bound to attract cops asking questions Travis didn't want to answer. He tried to rise enough to see his attackers, but more shots forced him back to a crouch. The boy's ghost remained, standing to one side and watching.

"Hey, kid." Travis looked right at the ghost, who seemed surprised to be seen.

Me?

Travis nodded. "Yeah. You got friends nearby?"

The ghost nodded. *Why?*

"Cause trouble for those guys to make them leave, and I'll send you on so you don't have to hang around here anymore." Travis couldn't promise heaven or that they would reunite with loved ones. That knowledge, he always joked, was above his pay grade. But he could give them rest. He had no way to know for certain, but he had the feeling that the ghost had been stuck here for a while.

You can do that? The boy looked wary.

"Yes. You can finally rest."

Will I see my grandma? the ghost asked.

Travis shook his head. "I don't know for sure. Maybe. You won't be here anymore."

Good enough, the ghost said and vanished. Travis slowed his pace to buy time, hoping the boy would keep his word.

He didn't have to wait long. Invisible feet kicked over the bottles and cans that lined nearby concrete steps, sending them flying with enough force to break glass.

"What the hell—" One of the men flinched at the sudden noise, looking around for reinforcements.

Empty beer cans levitated, then pelted Travis's attackers, hitting them in the head or smashing on the ground at their feet. Theatrical wailing added to the spooky effect.

"Fuck this shit, I'm gone." Two of the men ran down a side street.

The third man hesitated until a glass bottle crashed into a light pole right above his head, raining down shards. He fled without looking back.

Travis locked himself inside the Crown Vic. Within its wards, Travis felt himself relax knowing he was safe.

A small gang of ghosts appeared next to the driver's side window, laughing and joking with each other, proud of their success.

Pay up, mister. We're tired of being stuck here, the first boy said. The others looked expectantly at Travis, torn between hope and a history of being disappointed. Travis could guess their backstories; he heard similar tales from the men who stayed at St. Dismas. These were the ones who weren't lucky enough to survive.

Travis raised his hands and closed his eyes, confident that the would-be attackers were gone.

"Thank you," he told the ghosts. "It's time for you to move on to where you can rest in safety. Go into the light and find peace." In his mind's eye, he saw a shaft of light strike the road near where the ghosts gathered.

One by one, they walked toward the beam and vanished. The last to go was the boy who had first spoken to him. He turned back toward Travis with a wobbly smile, waved, and then followed the others into the light. It blinked out, and the street seemed much darker than before with its loss.

Travis seized the moment and drove off, ignoring the thudding of his heart and the shaking in his hands as he gripped the wheel.

Once he felt calmer, he called Brent. "I think we've got an evil gnome."

"Gnome?" Brent echoed. "I thought they were the cute little guys in old ladies' gardens."

"They come in all varieties, and one sort is definitely bad news." Travis gave Brent a brief recap.

"Yeah, that sounds like the kind of things people report around Mammoth Mine," Brent agreed when Travis finished. "But we're also looking at two sets of pissed-off ghosts; the ones who died in the actual explosions, and the ones who got killed by the Pinkertons in the strike a couple of months later."

"Maybe there's a way to get the ghosts to see the gnome as an enemy they can still punish for what happened to them," Travis mused. He took several deep breaths and did his best to let the tension drain from him.

"Are you okay? You sound a little off."

"There were three toughs waiting near the car when I came out of the library," Travis told him. "Ghosts helped me get rid of them, but if they had been stealthier, I might not have had a chance."

"You think it's whoever is hunting hunters?"

"Awfully big coincidence if it isn't." Travis still felt on edge, even though he was on the open highway and didn't see anything questionable around him.

"I know going to the library puts you in a bad place even without getting attacked," Brent said. "Want to grab lunch?"

Brent's offer made Travis smile, and he appreciated the kindness. "Thanks, but I'm due back at St. Dismas. I've been AWOL a lot lately, and with some of the hunts coming up, that's not likely to change."

"The invitation still stands," Brent told him. "Any time. Angela's traveling for work and then tacking on extra time away to visit family, so my social calendar is clear." Brent's girlfriend knew at least a little bit about his side gig hunting monsters, and supported him, although she didn't want to know all the details.

"Don't worry, I'll take you up on it when you least expect it." Travis already felt the shadows lighten. For all that Brent had his own nightmares and old scars, he always seemed to know how to help Travis out of a funk.

"When do you want to go to Mammoth Mine?" Brent asked. "I got caught up faster than I expected."

Before his vision at the library, Travis had been willing to take a few days before diving into a new hunt. What he experienced gave him a sense of urgency despite the fact that the disaster had occurred more than a hundred years ago.

"Tomorrow? Get it over with?"

"Yeah, that works," Brent agreed. "It's just down in Mount Pleasant. Not far. See you at ten?"

"Sure," Travis said. "And if you go out, watch your back."

"Will do," Brent promised.

Minutes later, Travis parked at the halfway house. Jon caught up to him by the time Travis reached his apartment.

"How did it go?" His priest friend gave a look of concern that warmed Travis's heart.

"There's buzz up in Mark's neck of the woods that someone is helping the monsters and making sure the hunters meet with accidents." Travis set his backpack down inside the doorway. "People are nervous, and they're seeing omens in their burnt toast. When I got back, there were some tough guys hanging around my car, but a pack of ghosts scared them off. I think the danger is real, but I'm not sure yet who's to blame."

"Troubling. How about the library?" Jon knew enough about Travis's checkered relationship with the Sinistram to understand the strain of even a routine visit to their facility.

"Stranger than usual." Travis poured a glass of water and offered one to Jon before he sat at the table. Jon joined him a moment later.

Jon listened as Travis talked about what he had learned, including the priest's incantation notebook and the vision.

"That's a lot for one afternoon," Jon replied.

"Yeah, but honestly, even the vision isn't the strangest thing," Travis said. "Whoever I get for a Keeper is always an asshole. That's part of the job, and it goes double because they don't like me. But someone removed all the vampire books, as well as several of the necromancy tomes. I don't believe that's coincidental. Whoever took them doesn't want anyone looking closely at vampire lore or raising the dead and undead."

"Interesting theory, but why?" Jon toyed with his glass as he spoke.

"I don't know, but I think we need to find out," Travis answered. "I've been going there for a long time, and an entire section never just vanished before. So...it's going to take some digging to figure out what's going on."

"Watch your back. Vampires don't like nosy humans interfering with their plans," Jon warned.

"Yeah, well. The Sinistram has tolerated mediums and psychics and people with magic, but they've never changed their position on vampires," Travis said. "It's always been canon that a monster is a monster is a monster. So, are we facing a vampire insurrection? Or have the powers that be decided vampires can be useful if properly... supervised."

"That's not likely to work out well," Jon observed.

"Probably not, but the kind of bureaucratic idiots who dream up things like that never have to handle the clean-up." Travis drained his water and felt a pang of regret at not having anything stronger available. The vision had left him badly shaken, and he knew Jon could probably tell.

"How about taking your mind off things for a while?" Jon suggested. "There's nothing more to be done tonight, and sometimes giving yourself a little space makes everything clearer. I have it on good authority that there's a bingo game that needs a caller."

Calling bingo was the last thing Travis really wanted to do, but he recognized the wisdom in Jon's suggestion and knew that if he stayed in his apartment, he would end up doing more research or phoning hunting contacts.

"I just happen to know a guy," Travis joked, and Jon grinned.

"Why don't you take a shower and wash away the day, then come down when you're ready," Jon said. "I left the invoices that I paid on your desk in the office. Dinner is haluski and mashed potatoes."

Travis liked their cook's version of the Eastern European dish, and his stomach growled.

"There's apple cobbler for dessert," Jon added as an inducement.

"Get thee behind me, Satan," Travis said with a laugh, although he wasn't up to fighting that particular temptation too hard.

Jon's phone alarm chimed. "That's my signal to go make sure everything is in order for tonight. See you once you get cleaned up."

A hot shower went a long way toward dispelling the tactile memories of the vision as well as the old book smell that always clung to his clothing when he visited the library. Tired as Travis was after the day's events, he knew that he needed the social aspect of going to the dining room for dinner, talking to their residents, and helping raise spirits with the bingo night.

He also knew that Jon and Matthew would probably drag him out of his apartment if he tried to renege.

Travis often ate in the dining room with St. Dismas's current residents. If the staff was shorthanded, he also pitched in to help serve the meal. Tonight, Jon waved him toward the line to get his tray and dinner.

"We've got it covered," Jon told him. "You've had a hard day. Go eat."

"Hey, Father Travis! There's a seat over here." Steve, one of the men who had been at the home longer than most, waved him over.

Travis carried his tray to the table and sat. "Just Travis these days," he reminded Steve. "I gave up the collar a long time ago."

Steve shrugged. "The stuff you do here with St. Dismas counts like a church. More than most churches," he said. Travis made a noncommittal response, not wanting to debate the matter.

"Do you believe in monsters?"

Steve's question caught Travis with a mouthful of food. He chewed a little slower, buying himself time to come up with an answer. "You mean really bad people?"

Steve shook his head. He was a burly man in his forties with a shaved head and tattoos that chronicled the highs and lows of his lifetime, from favorite bands to prison tats. He had made real progress leaving all that behind during his stay at St. Dismas. Travis didn't think that mere humans scared Steve.

"No. Monster-monsters. Maybe not like on TV. From the stories my nana used to tell us about the things that lived in the woods and the caves, back in the old country."

Travis regarded him seriously, ignoring the desire to brush off the discussion to gain an evening's peace. "Why?"

Steve looked around. No one else sat near them. He leaned forward and dropped his voice so only Travis could hear.

"There's word on the street about *things* out there in the shadows." Steve braced himself, ready not to be believed.

Travis met his gaze. "Tell me."

Steve fiddled with the rings on his fingers. "There are always ghosts. Everyone knows that. Worse some places than others, but anyone who's been on the street for long has crosses, crucifixes, and salt to make the ghosts leave them alone. Works better on some than others."

Travis had picked up as much from working with their clients at St. Dismas. Some of the men shied away from the topic when it came up, but even then, he could see in their eyes that they believed, but either couldn't face their fear or were wary of admitting it.

"I know. I see them too." Travis didn't say much to their residents about his abilities, and they knew nothing of his monster hunting with Brent, but validating Steve's report was likely to get the man to say more.

Steve ran one hand over the other. "You do? Huh... Is it a sin?"

"To see them? I don't believe that," Travis said. "Not everyone agrees. But the ghosts didn't ask to be that way. Still part of the flock."

"Okay," Steve said to himself, running his tongue over his lips. "Some of the ghosts ignore us. Others try to help—warning about the cops or bad guys, but there are some dangerous ones—we pass the word around and steer clear."

He cleared his throat and glanced from side to side again, not wanting to be overheard. "But the *monsters* have been getting worse."

"What kind of monsters do you mean?" Travis knew that many of their guests had a history of addiction and psychological problems. That might make him doubt their accounts. But Steve had been at St. Dismas long enough to get treatment.

"Black dogs with red eyes that just appear and disappear, some-times they carry people away," Steve replied in a voice above a whis-per. "Little ugly creatures with big teeth that steal food. An old woman who offers to tell your fortune and sucks out your soul."

When we've handled the mine monsters, Brent and I have to handle some clean-up closer to home, Travis thought, chagrinned they hadn't noticed. He and Brent periodically went on patrol, but it had been a while, and he promised himself that he would create a regular schedule.

"There are more of them? Showing up in more places?" Travis prompted.

Steve nodded. "Yeah, I heard through the grapevine that a couple of my old buddies went missing. A few days later, they found bones and clothing. Something *ate* them."

The monsters were smart enough to prey on people the cops were unlikely to believe, roaming the alleys and back streets that even the police avoided.

"I'll see what I can do about it," Travis promised him. "Do you have a theory about why it's worse lately?"

Steve gave a humorless laugh. "Not really. Full moon, no moon, holiday, none of that seems to matter. Some of the guys banded together, managed to get some guns and knives. They were ex-military, knew how to fight. They started to patrol, and word went out for the rest of us to stay inside the area. For a while, that helped."

"Then what?" Travis feared he could guess.

"The monsters got them," Steve replied. "Almost like they leveled up against the threat and ripped them apart. Since then, people just hide. They don't fight unless they're cornered and then they lose."

"You're safe here." Travis didn't elaborate on the supernatural protections around St. Dismas, from spells to salt lines to sigils and wards. Now, he wondered if the halfway house might be targeted because of those precautions by whatever was sending the monsters.

No, he thought. *Not whatever. Whoever. Just like how the monster hunters are being hunted. Sinistram's the only group powerful enough to pull off a city-wide monsterpalooza. But what's in it for them?*

"Thanks for listening, Padre," Steve picked up his tray. "If you have any friends on the witchy side who could help, my boys on the street would sure appreciate it."

"See you at bingo?" Travis asked when Steve stood. "I'm calling tonight. Don't let that scare you off."

Steve laughed. "Save a seat for me. I might just make it."

Travis watched him leave and replayed their conversation in his mind.

The Sinistram has done its best to be invisible for a long time. It's not like they're signing their work, but those in the know are likely to suspect them first. So how does super-charging monsters and killing monster hunters serve a purpose? I'm missing something big. I just don't know how to fill in the gap.

Travis found that presiding over the bingo night jostled him out of his thoughts and lifted his mood. No money was exchanged, everyone got cards and chits for free, and the cookie prizes came from donations or the St. Dismas kitchen. Still, even their most streetwise residents got into the spirit of the game, hooting and hollering and going all-in.

Afterward, movie night provided an action flick and snacks, a popular way to pass the evening.

"Nicely done," he told Jon as they stood in the back of the common room, watching the middle of the movie. "You set everything up to come off without a hitch."

Jon shrugged, although he smiled at the praise. "Nothing new or different, but it's worth it when they get some time to take a load off. And you were an awesome bingo caller."

"We used to joke that a class in bingo games, bake sales, potluck dinners, and yard sales would have stood us in better stead as parish priests than some of the high-level theology," Travis replied.

Or how to step in and be the town's mine witch. They left that out at school, too.

He gestured for Jon to step outside the room with him. "Your family's been in Pittsburgh for a while, right? Any of them work in the mines?"

Jon nodded. "Back in the day. Like around World War Two."

"Anyone ever mention mine witches?"

Jon raised an eyebrow. "Let me guess. You and Brent are cleaning up old messes again?"

"When aren't we?"

"Fair enough." Jon thought for a moment. "The people who worked the mines were very old when I was a kid. By then, the underground mines were closed, and there were just a couple of strip mines left. But sometimes at the holidays, the old men would sit around and drink and tell stories. If I stayed real quiet under the table, they forgot I was there, and they'd tell some doozies."

"I bet."

"They were all good Catholics, but they also believed in ghosts, monsters, and witches," Jon replied. "Just like the women would go to church to pray in the morning and stop at the tea shop to consult the neighborhood seer on their way home."

The official term Travis had learned in seminary was "syncretism," the blending of different belief systems. People saw nothing wrong with hedging their bets, since good luck often seemed elusive.

"What did they say about the witches?"

Jon took a moment to answer. "Geez, I haven't thought about that stuff for a long while. But they'd tell stories about close calls: cave-ins, rock falls, bad air, fires. Sometimes there was a ghost warning them to get out. Other times, they swore a monster caused the problem. They all wore saints' medallions and took omens seriously. And they thought they were safer because witches from the old country put spells on the mines."

"Did they ever say what the witch actually did?" Travis told him briefly about what he had found at the library.

Jon nodded. "That sounds right. They mentioned how the witch would bless the mine and cast out demons and unholy creatures. Never heard them repeat what the witch said, but I got the feeling it was more of an incantation and less of a prayer. Interesting that from what you found, sometimes they got both a witch and a priest in one package."

That hadn't surprised Travis, since he felt sure he wasn't the only one who had ever combined his religion with the natural power of inherent magic.

"Does that help?" Jon asked.

"Yeah, it does. Validating a theory," Travis replied. "Thanks."

"Oh, Aricella said she was coming by tomorrow morning with the bakery order, and she made a point of saying that she wanted to talk to you," Jon added.

Aricella was a talented bruja in addition to being a mighty fine baker. She was one of the folks Travis had dubbed his "Night Vigil"—people with magic or supernatural gifts who served as an intelligence network, reporting anything unusual their talents revealed.

The unlikely band of informants had provided valuable tips more than once that had helped Travis avert trouble or find the missing piece for a hunt.

"Let me know when she gets here," Travis replied. "I haven't seen her in a while."

When the movie ended, everyone helped clean the snack table and stack the folding chairs. St. Dismas kept a nightly curfew, another way to add structure to their guests' lives and make it easier for them to avoid bad influences on their own outside the facility.

Afterward, Travis got ready for bed, which normally included time spent clearing his mind with meditation and prayer. While he had been iffy about praying since he left the priesthood, he found the familiar words and cadences soothing, and figured that any worth-while cosmic entity would understand his struggle.

Most of the time, the combination of a dark, quiet room, soft music, and contemplation helped to still his racing thoughts and relax tight shoulders. Some nights, it wasn't enough. He gave up after half an hour and went to make himself a cup of tea.

Resigned, Travis checked the police reports of missing persons, and then shifted to the social media sites where loved ones posted looking for information. He had learned long ago that the unofficial bulletin boards were more accurate than the police information.

Pittsburgh's missing persons count didn't compare to larger cities like Los Angeles, for which Travis remained thankful. Many people were found fairly quickly, although a few well-known cases remained unsolved. Travis started counting the recent postings, separating them by the date reported. Sure enough, the numbers had increased over the last year. The numbers weren't large enough to attract media attention, but Travis saw a definite upward trend.

More worrisome were the number of disappearances that appeared completely random, people who just vanished without any history of financial or personal trouble.

Like they've been snatched. But why? And who took them?

Aside from their lack of predictable reasons to run away, Travis couldn't find any other common elements. They were male and female, representing a range of ages and ethnicities. The only thing he noted was an absence of both children and elderly people, two groups that usually figured prominently in missing persons lists.

Travis yawned and figured the tea had finally done its job. He made some final notes on his findings and closed down his computer. He fell asleep quickly, but his dreams were dark.

CHAPTER FOUR

"ARICELLA, wonderful to see you. Please, come in and have a cup of coffee." Travis was with Jon when the baker came to the halfway house kitchen door.

The slim, dark-haired woman wore an open flannel shirt over a tee in the cool morning air, with jeans and baker's clogs. "Jon, Travis, glad to see you too. I brought these for the residents, and that little one on top is for us." Aricella handed over a stack of boxes that were still warm on the bottom and smelled wonderful.

They went to the kitchen, and Jon brought three cups of coffee to the table with fixings. He put the large boxes on the counter and brought the extra one to share.

Travis took a rapturous inhale as Jon opened the box to reveal a mix of pan dulce and house-made churros.

"These look amazing." He knew from experience they would taste just as good.

Aricella's cheeks pinked at the praise and she grinned. "I figured everyone could use a sugar boost."

For several moments, they savored the treats, sipped their coffee, and exchanged neighborhood news. Travis thought Aricella looked tired.

"Have you noticed anything strange lately?" she finally asked.

"Gotta define strange," Travis replied. "We have a pretty broad range."

Aricella knew some of what he and Brent did, and lent her own magical protections to help. "Stranger than usual." She ran a finger around the lip of her coffee cup. "I put down protections around the bakery, and I've got a thriving side gig with charms, amulets, and wards for clients and the neighbors. People are jittery."

Travis and Jon exchanged a look.

"Anything happen recently?" Jon asked as he refilled her cup, and Aricella took a few sips before she continued.

"The ghosts are more restless than usual," Aricella said. "Some of them have gotten troublesome, but with the others, it's like there's been a shift that has them riled up. What scares ghosts?"

"How can you tell a difference?" Travis asked.

"More chatter on the street about hauntings," Aricella replied. "More requests for banishment rituals and charms. People talking about bad omens, crows, black cats, and that weird black moon. And it's not just ghosts. There've been more sightings of *creatures* than in a long time."

"Pittsburgh is a very old town. There's been a lot of history here for ghosts—and monsters—to set up shop," Travis observed.

Aricella shook her head. "This feels different, but I can't quite put it into words. Like something has woken up what was sleeping and turned them loose."

"What kind of creatures?" Jon asked while Travis mulled over her last statement.

"Black dogs. Women in white. Bridge trolls. Boo hags. And it's not just my folks seeing them. I know other neighborhood witches—Italian, Slavic, Black. It's happening everywhere."

"Are people getting hurt, or just frightened?" Travis asked.

"So far, just scared, but what happens when someone has a heart attack or falls down the steps or gets in a car accident because of what they've seen?" Aricella challenged. "None of us can figure out what's turned up the volume, but if this keeps up, I'll be spending more time doing the witchy side of my business than baking."

"I'll keep my ears and eyes open." Travis added Aricella's neighborhood to the list of streets around St. Dismas that needed more protection. He knew that he and Brent couldn't protect every alley in the city, but a good cleansing could often drive out dark entities for a while until they regrouped.

And if their hunch was right and the uptick in spectral activity was being caused intentionally, getting rid of the cause would go a long way toward reducing the incidents.

"Thank you." Aricella finished her coffee and set the cup aside. "I know you can't be everywhere, but I figured you would want to know. Anything you can do to help is much appreciated."

Travis and Jon walked her to the door, and conversation turned back to the weather. When she was gone, Jon gave him a look. "I'm guessing that meant more to you than what I probably got out of it?"

Travis nodded. "Yeah. I'm afraid it's part of the problem that Steve told us about. And if it's also linked to the issues up in Mark Wojcik's area, then we've got to take a good look at who is powerful enough to make that much trouble and figure out why." He shook his head. "I really prefer small, easily-fixed problems to mini-apocalypses."

Jon clapped him on the shoulder. "Can't blame you on that. You out with Brent again today?"

"Yeah. Might not be back in time for dinner depending on how things go."

"We've got you covered," Jon replied. "Although I have it on good authority that it's spaghetti night with the cook's grandmother's sauce recipe, so I can't guarantee there will be leftovers."

<hr>

"IF THEY HAD ALL these big mine fires and collapses, why weren't there more protests?" Brent asked as Travis drove toward what was left of the town of Mammoth and its coal mine.

"There were," Travis replied, "About three months after the Mammoth disaster, there was a huge march by a thousand workers on the Morewood Works, another nearby mine. The local police fired into the crowd, killing nine of them, and the officers were acquitted. The law and the powers-that-be weren't on the side of the workers."

Brent's sour expression made his feelings clear.

"Did you look at those videos I sent you, with the urban explorer who went into the Mammoth Mine?" Travis asked.

"Yeah, he's either brave or crazy," Brent agreed. "The whole place looked like it could come down on his head at any moment."

The Mammoth Mine had actually been two mines, a shaft mine and a slope mine. Parts of it had continued to operate even after the 1907 explosion that killed over one hundred miners, not closing for good until 1927. At the time, there had been a huge setup including massive brick coke ovens, breakers, and tipples, along with rail lines and engines.

"It did look pretty sketchy." Travis shuddered. "I was surprised that the mine company left so much equipment behind. Rail cars, drills, all kinds of specialized tools. Just abandoned."

"A lot of it was big stuff," Brent pointed out. "Getting it out and moving it somewhere else wouldn't have been easy."

"Yeah, but the buddies of the guys who owned the mine owned the railroad. I guess they just didn't care," Travis replied.

"We're not going inside, right?" Brent double-checked. He couldn't help sounding a little nervous. The explorer's footage of twisted metal, gaping deep holes, dark tunnels, and rock slides had brought out a claustrophobia he hadn't realized existed.

Travis chuckled. "No. The mine entrances have been blocked off completely now. And even if they weren't, we take enough risks without asking for trouble. But from the videos, it's only been a couple of years since people could get at least some of the way inside."

"Is there anything left around the mine?" Brent couldn't help being curious. "And what does 'coke' have to do with anything?"

"They superheated coal to refine it into a harder substance called coke, which was used in iron and steel manufacturing," Travis said. "I guess I watched a few more videos than you did."

Travis glanced at the GPS on his phone before he went on. "There were massive ovens near the mine to refine the coal to coke, but those are gone now, along with the other big buildings that got the coal out of the mine and broke it up. There's a concrete dynamite shack, a boiler house, and a gigantic man-made mountain of slate they used to call a boney pile."

"Did anyone get in trouble for the disaster?" Brent figured he already knew the answer, but he needed to ask.

"Not really. The mine inspector had just cleared the mine as safe days before. People are still arguing over whether the inspection missed something big or whether the explosive and suffocating gases seeped in through cracks in the rocks," Travis said. "But of course, the owners weren't liable."

They passed a granite marker and a historic location sign, turning off the main road onto a paved driveway that led to a large expanse of green lawn with the old boiler house at one end.

Brent spotted the boney pile right away, looming gray and ugly in the background. Over to the side, he saw where an entrance to the mine had been sealed up.

"The news reports said that when the explosion happened, there were bodies strewn over sixty acres," Travis said. "They were burned, crushed by rock falls, and slammed into the walls. Many couldn't be identified. The company buried them in two long trenches."

"Shit. No wonder the place is haunted." On such a bright, sunny day, it was difficult for Brent to reconcile the horrific history with the peaceful green hills.

"Can you sense them?" Brent asked after he parked and they got out.

Travis concentrated, closing his eyes. "They're out there, but they're hanging back," he said after a few quiet moments.

"What about the gnome? Do you think it played a role in the disaster?" Brent asked.

"I don't know. It could have moved in after the people left," Travis replied. "There were enough dangers that mines didn't necessarily need monsters to make them explode. The carnage would have been a feast for any creature close enough to gorge itself."

Brent nodded. "If they kept the mine going, the gnome could probably snack a little at a time. Once the mine closed, did it go to sleep? Did the explorers wake it up? Is it getting by on what it can grab from hikers, hunters, and explorers?"

Travis shrugged. "Maybe. For all we know, it left and came back again. But it's here now, people are getting killed, and we need to get rid of it."

"Does any of this look like your vision?" Brent asked.

Travis shook his head. "No. The entrance is all wrong. So I still have no idea what I saw or why it matters."

As they drew closer to the mouth of the old mine, Brent felt a cold breeze and caught a whiff of stale air.

"Look there." He grabbed Travis by the shoulder and pointed. "Something's opened the entrance."

They moved closer with their weapons ready. "And it sure looks like the digging came from *inside*," Travis pointed out, and Brent saw how the dirt fell, and the ragged opening definitely looked like it had been dug by something *in* the tunnel.

"That explains how it got out," Brent said. "But what woke it up? Because the deaths have all been in the last few months...and nothing for long periods before that."

"It might go dormant for a time and then become active again. Either that, or someone intentionally reactivated it," Travis replied. "I like the first explanation better, but given what we've seen elsewhere, I'm afraid the second is more likely to be right."

Brent laid down a large salt and iron filing line that encircled the mine opening. Travis set out an offering of whiskey and cheese inside the circle.

"I hope it's hungry," Brent said as Travis placed the last of the bait to draw the monster out of the mine.

"The ghosts are watching," Travis told him. Brent couldn't see the spirits, but he felt observed.

"I don't see any of the recent victims in the crowd," Travis added. "Ready?"

Brent nodded and shouldered his shotgun, filled with rock salt rounds.

Travis spoke the incantation he had copied at the Sinistram library to summon and bind the gnome. At first, nothing happened. Brent wondered if the creature had moved on or fallen back asleep.

A deep growl sounded from inside the mine, and the gnome burst free in a spray of dirt and loose rock. It stood roughly the height of a fire hydrant, with a similar stocky profile, and was covered in pale, leathery skin. Powerful arms and legs protruded from a squat, muscular, naked body with clawed feet and hands. It had a flattened face and small eyes, with a mouth filled with rows of sharp, pointed teeth, and it confronted Travis and Brent with a deafening howl.

Travis chanted his spell to permanently banish the gnome and created an unseen barrier to keep the monster from rushing them. He threw one of his flash-bangs to slow it down and buy himself more time. The fire and protective additions only distracted the gnome for a moment before it came at them again.

After their run-in with the tommyknocker, Brent had brought some heavier firepower this time. He fired a non-explosive armor-piercing round from their grenade launcher, augmented with iron and salt. It struck the gnome in the chest, tearing a ragged hole that still did not stop the creature's attack.

The wounded gnome threw itself at the invisible barrier, shrieking in anger when it couldn't break through.

Brent fired again, aiming for the gnome's head, but it dodged just in time and roared.

Travis kept chanting, and the gnome focused on the sound, turning to face him and shrieking again before it dropped to all fours and began to dig, trying to get under the magical boundary.

The ground crumbled, breaking the barrier, and the gnome came at Brent faster than he thought possible.

"Oh, hell no!" Brent fired again and knocked the gnome onto its back. "Chant faster!"

Brent's shots didn't keep the gnome down for long, even though it oozed ichor from several wounds. Solid and heavy despite its small size, the gnome tackled Brent, knocking the grenade launcher out of reach and pinning him down. Sharp claws dug into Brent's arms and thighs, and it was all he could do to keep the vicious teeth from his throat. Pain lanced through his bad leg.

The air around Brent suddenly dropped to freezing as the mine ghosts entered the fight and made themselves visible. They wrapped around Brent and the gnome, keeping them apart as Travis's voice rose above the clamor.

The gnome snapped at the ghosts but didn't let go of Brent. Massed together, the spirits had the strength to show themselves and to keep the gnome from sinking its teeth into Brent, but he didn't know how long they could keep up their barrier.

Brent struggled to free his dagger. He pulled it loose and rammed it into the gnome's belly, sinking the blade to the hilt.

"Return to the darkness from which you have come!" Travis commanded as the spell wound to its conclusion. "Sleep in the deep places and do not awaken."

The gnome's grip faltered. Brent bucked under it, feeling the claws rip free, as magic and the ghosts sent the creature backward to the mine entrance. It vanished into the hole and did not reemerge as Travis shouted the last words of the spell.

The ghosts swept away from Brent toward the mine. He didn't know whether they meant to chase the gnome deeper into the tunnels or just keep it inside.

"Brent!" Travis ran to where Brent lay and gave him a once-over, assessing the damage the troll had caused.

"Seal the mine. I won't bleed out that fast." Brent gritted his teeth. "Don't let that son of a bitch get back out."

Travis looked conflicted for a moment, then nodded. Brent knew his friend's first instinct was to protect him, but they would be in trouble if the gnome rallied for a second round.

Travis hurled one of his modified flash-bangs into the mine to drive the creature farther into the tunnels and got out of the way in case it caused a rockfall or set anything inside on fire. When that didn't happen, he breathed a sigh of relief and hoped that would keep the creature away from the mouth of the tunnel long enough for him to seal it up.

He grabbed the bucket of ready-mix cement they had brought and returned for a couple of cement blocks they had also carried in. Both the mix and the blocks were treated with a combination of ritual elements designed to create and hold a binding on whatever they enclosed.

Brent worked as quickly as he could, ignoring the pain, and fixing the blocks in place to seal the entrance. Then he covered them and the entire front of the opening in the quick-drying mixture. Travis spoke a litany of binding commands as he worked, and to Brent's relief, the ghosts did not try to stop him.

When he finished, Travis returned to Brent and checked the punctures where the gnome had grabbed him.

"You need to see Matthew again and make sure those don't get some freaky gnome infection." Travis tried to lighten the moment. "They probably hurt like a mother, but there's not a lot of tearing, and they don't look as deep as they probably feel. Although you're going to be riding home in your boxers."

"They felt like he was going straight through the bone," Brent said through the pain as Travis helped him to his feet. His bad leg hurt, but it held his weight. Brent looked over toward the mine. "Do you think what we did will hold him?"

"I hope so," Travis said. "We'll check back in a few weeks. But I do wonder what people will make of the cement."

"Given the attacks, it might not seem mysterious," Brent said, "although they might question who did it." Travis stayed close to him, and they headed back to the car.

"How bad is it?" Travis asked after he had done what he could to wipe off the wounds with antiseptic and bind them enough to stop the bleeding.

Brent shifted in his seat. "I've had a lot worse. Uncomfortable, but not terrible." Time in the military had taught him an entirely new scale for what hurt. "And of course, it's the leg I already fucked up." A long-ago shattered bone left Brent with screws and pins, and a leg that functioned but ached when it rained.

"Did I imagine it, or were the ghosts fighting the gnome?" Travis changed the subject.

"They definitely were, just like with the tommyknocker," Brent confirmed. "The spirits were able to make themselves visible, and they kept trying to get between me and the gnome and throw it off. Which makes me question the accounts we heard."

Travis nodded. "Someone could misunderstand and think the ghosts were attacking them instead of being protective, but I think you're right that the people who were attacked and killed weren't hurt by the ghosts. And now that the gnome is locked up again and hopefully asleep, there shouldn't be any more casualties."

"Which makes me wonder about the two hunters who died near here in a car wreck. We were quick to think the ghosts caused a problem, but what if it wasn't either the ghosts or the gnome? What if whoever summoned the gnome was watching and playing backup?" Brent asked.

"Shit," Travis muttered as they buckled in, and he turned around. "Then I'm gonna need to ask you to ride shotgun and help me, in case whoever-that-is has some sort of way to know if someone is near the mine."

"I didn't see any security cameras."

"If they used magic, they wouldn't need it," Travis replied. "And that's likely, since whoever is causing the problems is tied in somewhere to the supernatural community."

Nothing had tried to stop them on the way in. The Crown Vic had its own protections, marked in hidden places with sigils and warded with protection and distraction spells. That should have made it easy to evade any arcane traps set to stop hunters who survived the gnome.

But as they neared the top of the approach road, the car suddenly jerked toward a stand of old trees, their thick trunks scarred from the last fatal crash.

"Grab the wheel!" Travis shouted.

Brent lurched toward the driver's side to wrestle for control as Travis slammed on the brakes and shouted words of power.

The car fishtailed, taking all of Brent's strength to keep them on the road as Travis spoke defensive spells. At this speed, the big trees would make a mess even of the heavy steel in the Crown Vic. Worse, Brent thought he glimpsed rocks and a ravine.

Travis chanted and Brent swore. It felt like invisible hands fought for control of the steering wheel as Brent felt the strain in his shoulders and arms.

Just when Brent felt certain that he was losing the battle, the force vanished. Travis's hands joined his on the wheel as they corrected to keep from slewing across the other lane and into the trees. The maneuver slammed them into each other and threw Travis into the door.

"Hang on," Travis warned. He kept driving for another mile or so, but when nothing else tried to kill them, he eased off the side of the road and put the car in park.

Both men were wide-eyed and breathing hard from the near miss.

Travis slowly relaxed his white-knuckled grip on the wheel,

ready to grab it again. "Well, now we know what killed the other hunters." He willed his heart to stop pounding.

"That's gotta be magic," Brent said. "There wasn't anything on the road to make us lurch."

"I'll see about getting some of our witch friends out here to un-hex whatever caused the wrecks," Travis said.

When they reached the main road without incident, Brent let out the breath he had been holding. "Whoever set that wanted to give the gnome the first shot at killing them, and finish the job if necessary," Brent said, feeling the attack in sore muscles and new, bleeding wounds, although it was a toss-up whether the cuts from the tommy-knocker or the punctures from the gnome hurt more.

"Maybe you should get some body armor," Travis said. "To help you keep the blood on the inside."

Brent flipped him off, but without heat. "You could be right."

TRAVIS CALLED AHEAD, so Matthew was waiting for them when they arrived. Brent looked over to Travis. "I appreciate the concern, but it's not like I need to be wheeled in on a gurney."

"I'll be the judge of that," Matthew joked, although Brent saw the concern in his eyes. His mouth tightened into a line when he took in the holes in Brent's clothing and the blood. "Come on. Let's see how bad it is."

Brent knew the way to the infirmary. At this time of day, St. Dismas was quiet, so they avoided questioning looks from the residents.

Sheer stubbornness meant Brent got himself onto the table. He managed to get his shirt off, although the wounds in both arms made movement painful.

Matthew examined the punctures closely, frowning as he gently poked and prodded. "I don't know whether to be glad it was claws instead of teeth or not. They both carry risks for infection. Fortunately, these look pretty clean. Although I don't know what sort of germs a gnome might carry."

The medic flushed the wounds and applied a tincture and salve that Brent knew had been specially compounded for supernaturally-caused injuries. "I'm hoping that gets them healing quickly without any infection," Matthew said as he bandaged the wounds. "The good thing about bleeding—up to a point—is that it can help clean out the wound too."

He went to a cupboard and poured pills into a prescription bottle. "These should help with the pain so you get good sleep," he told Brent as he handed it over. "I know you're not going to like hearing this, but I think you need to take some time off from hunting—at least a couple of days—so this wound and the last one actually have time to heal."

"How do you feel?" Travis asked, handing Brent a pair of sweat-pants from the donation pile.

"Like I was clawed by a gnome," Brent replied, deadpan. "I'll be fine."

"Let's take a couple of days for research, and then there's another haunting I want to check out," Travis said. "There was a circus train that overturned a hundred years ago, and apparently the ghosts of the animals are causing problems."

Brent knew his friend was saving his ego by giving him time to heal. "That's a new one." He paused, worried. "I appreciate a chance to get fixed up, but someone is still killing hunters out there."

"Yep. And there's no point in tempting fate by going in at less than a hundred percent," Travis countered.

Brent glared at him, knowing Travis was right but still feeling guilty about being the cause of the slowdown. "All right, but I'm going to research the hell out of this while I'm sidelined."

Travis and Matthew exchanged an exasperated look. "We're only talking a couple of days, not weeks," Travis reminded him. "I know you could probably white-knuckle it if you had to, but it's not that dire, yet."

"Hunters who take decent care of themselves live to shoot monsters longer," Matthew observed. "I think I read that from a fortune cookie."

Brent sighed, knowing that he was outnumbered. "Okay. But just a couple of days."

"Don't get an infection, and we'll go from there," Travis said.

"You two are a real handful, you know that?" Matthew said with exasperated fondness. "Go home. Sleep. Both of you."

"Give me my keys," Brent said.

Travis shook his head. "Not tonight. Sleep here, enjoy the painkillers, and tomorrow if Matthew clears you, you can go home then. Free room, clean sheets, and a hot breakfast. It's a pretty good deal."

Brent was too tired and sore to argue, and he knew Travis's concern came from the heart. "Fine. But only because you threw in breakfast."

———

THANKS TO THE PAINKILLERS, Brent slept hard, barely waking in time to catch the end of the promised breakfast. Scrambled eggs, bacon, and toast lifted his mood and his energy. He did his best not to show that the injuries still hurt when Matthew checked him over, but he doubted that the medic was fooled.

"Healing nicely, no sign of infection," Matthew told him. "You're cleared to drive." He handed him a bottle with a few pills inside. "Take these in case you need them to sleep for the next couple of nights. They won't be an issue with your usual prescription pain meds for that leg, but don't mix with alcohol. Try not to get punctured by any monsters until you heal up."

"Thank you." Brent appreciated Matthew's expertise and good humor. "I'll call Travis later. I have some leads I want to run down—by phone," he assured Matthew. "In my nice, safe desk chair."

Once he was back home, Brent made a pot of coffee and set up his laptop and a notepad so he could make calls and research from the comfort of his couch.

He settled in and called Mark Wojcik. "What are you hearing through the Occulatum?" Brent asked after a brief greeting, knowing that Mark was connected to the more moderate organization of researchers.

"Hello to you, too," Mark replied jovially. "Did you fight the gnome yet?"

"Yeah, clawed me up some. I'm cooling my heels until I get cleared for active duty." Brent gave Mark a short version of the fight.

"Damn. That's a new one. But for what it's worth, I think you're right about the gnome either finding the mine on its own or being drawn there. And I really don't like the possibilities from the second option."

"Are your contacts running into anything similar? Dormant monsters creating new problems? Have there been any more hunter deaths?" In the background, a car engine turned off, and Brent realized he had caught Mark in his garage.

"No deaths, but a couple of near-misses that are hard to believe were accidents," Mark said. "Father Leo and I have been getting the word out to all the hunters we know to watch their backs."

"If we're right about someone using monsters to draw out the hunters, then until we figure this out, there's no such thing as a cold haunt. Whoever's behind this has enough magic to wake up a gnome, so that means they can probably juice up banished ghosts or call new monsters," Brent said. "But we still don't know why."

"One of those near-misses happened when someone sabotaged the hunters' truck while they were fighting some angry ghosts. Last I checked, most ghosts couldn't cut brake lines," Mark added. "Then two other hunters were nearly taken out with rifle shots. Luckily, they were psychic and literally saw it coming, but it's not deer season, if you know what I mean."

"A deer rifle can hit a target that's about 300 feet away, can't it?" Brent's experience was more with military weaponry.

"Technically, yes," Mark answered. "Although most people go for around 100 feet."

"Still, that's far enough away to make it difficult to see the shooter," Brent mused.

"That's sort of the point," Mark said. "As for the Occulatum, they're worried. Not just about the weird omen stuff and the threats to hunters, but I get the feeling there's political church stuff going on. Even Father Leo has been on edge."

"Do you think he'd answer a direct question if you asked?"

"Depends. What do you want to know?" Mark asked.

"Whether he thinks Sinistram might be involved," Brent said.

"You don't mince words." Mark blew out a breath. "I can ask. I know Father Leo tries to stay away from those sorts, like Travis does. I take it Travis has suspicions, and he can't look into them because the Sons of Darkness still hold a grudge?"

"Yep. He got weird vibes when he went to the library a few days ago, and a bunch of books were missing from the shelves, but the priests wouldn't tell him anything," Brent said.

"Books on what?"

"Vampires, mostly. And a few on necromancers."

"Well, that can't be good," Mark replied. "Why would vampires be involved?"

"We're still trying to figure that out," Brent admitted. "Which was another thing I was hoping you and Father Leo could do some poking around to get intel."

"I'll keep my ears open and let you know what I hear," Mark promised.

"If you have any other names of recently dead hunters you haven't had a chance to look into, send them to me since I'm sidelined for a day or two. I can see what shows up in my system." As a licensed detective, Brent had access to specialized databases.

"Will do," Mark said. "Keep your head down and try not to piss off any more gnomes."

Brent ended the call and refilled his coffee cup, fortifying himself for the next call. He couldn't spike his drink to ease the tension, and the painkiller didn't really cover anxiety.

"Fuck," he muttered under his breath, and called one of the people he disliked most.

"Brent. What a surprise. To what can I attribute the honor?" Shane, Brent's CHARON contact, answered with the same slippery charm that always grated on Brent's nerves.

"Who's killing hunters, and what do vampires have to do with it?"

Shane was silent for a moment, long enough to make Brent suspect that Shane might be surprised that Brent knew something, but not that he found the question unlikely.

"You've been watching too much TV," Shane finally replied, but his condescension didn't sound as cocksure as usual.

"Here's a theory. Tell me if you've heard it," Brent said. "Someone is waking up dormant monsters and luring hunters to deal with them in order to put a hit on the hunters if the monsters don't kill them."

"There's therapy for those kinds of delusions, Brent."

Yeah, he definitely sounds a little shaken. "Is CHARON behind it? You've never cared much for hunters who don't play for your team." Brent found himself holding his breath.

"Freelance hunters are unruly, undisciplined loose cannons that pose as much danger to themselves and bystanders as they do the monsters," Shane replied, slipping into the company line Brent had heard before. "But it's a stretch to suggest that we've put a contract out on them."

"Has someone else? Because there's too much going on to be coincidental, and when I think of bureaucratic, immoral, powerful organizations that wouldn't blink at offing people who got in their way, CHARON is at the top of the list."

"Oh, we're all of that," Shane replied. "But in this particular case, we aren't involved. You can take that as meaning we aren't involved because there is no conspiracy, or because someone else's team has the ball, but it's the truth."

For one of the only times in their long, acrimonious relationship, Brent believed him. "Are vampires behind it?"

Shane's pause was longer this time. "What do you know?" His voice had lost its humor and dropped into a deeper, more dangerous tone.

"How about I tell you a story?" Brent pushed his luck. "Someone with money, connections, and power wants to be rid of rabble hunters so they can operate more freely. They lure hunters onto ginned-up hunts to cull the numbers with plausible deniability. Meanwhile, they broker a deal with the rich, immortal monsters—aka vampires— who want to run their business enterprises hunter-free, for a cut."

"Interesting story," Shane said. "Got proof?"

"Working on it. Can you prove me wrong?"

Shane gave an exaggerated sigh. "You know, if there is such a plot —and that's a very big, unlikely 'if'—calling the people you think might be involved puts a huge target on your back."

"Sometimes you need bait to draw the monster out of its lair," Brent said. "If it isn't CHARON, is Sinistram behind it?"

"Join us and you'll be safer," Shane said. "The offer still stands."

"Still no," Brent countered. "I know you guys in the secret soci- eties talk, after you compare your decoder rings and club handshakes. So what have you heard?"

Brent could picture Shane seething, and it was a bright spot in an otherwise suckish day.

"The less powerful vamps have been lying low more than usual," Shane finally said. "Wish we could take credit for it, but we can't. The top fanger brass has pretty well fallen off the map—they have their hidden society, and they're aware we know about it. We had a truce. They don't slaughter people, and we don't wipe them out."

"Since I don't think even you could cover up a wholesale vampire massacre, I'm guessing the truce hasn't been broken," Brent replied.

"Yet."

For the first time, Brent heard a note of fear in Shane's voice.

"You think there's something in the works?" Brent was afraid Shane would remember who he was talking to and clam up before he said something important.

"Just a hunch. And since a bunch of us are psychic, that counts for something," Shane replied. "People are taking omens seriously, that black moon, and then the lunar eclipse. Weird power outages and more reports of shadow creatures than usual. Don't know whether that matters or not. But *if* something was in the works, killing off hunters would help avoid being interrupted."

"Good point, but why pick us off instead of going after the monster special forces, that's what CHARON sees itself as, right?" Brent asked. "You're organized, professional, and armed to the teeth. We're a rag-tag bunch of guys with rifles and salt. Why go after us?"

Shane didn't answer, and Brent felt the unspoken reply like a gut punch. "Oh my God. They wouldn't have to, if CHARON is already compromised," Brent said in a voice barely above a whisper.

"I didn't say that," Shane defended. "I just patiently listened to your theory to be helpful."

His lack of an outspoken denial was worse than if he launched into a heated defense.

"Thanks. You've actually helped a lot." Brent ended the call before Shane could get in a snarky reply. He sat there for several moments, staring at the phone in his hand, processing the conversation.

Shit. He as much as admitted that either CHARON is already involved, or that they might not side with the hunters if something happens. If that's true, they're not the ones in charge, which leans into Sinistram taking the lead. But what's in it for them? And where do the vampires figure into it?

Brent's email pinged, and he saw a new message from Mark with the list of hunters he had requested. Brent pushed worries about vampire conspiracies out of his mind for the moment, made a fresh pot of coffee, and dug into the comforting routine of data searching.

An hour later, he called Travis, who answered on the second ring.

"Why aren't you sleeping?" Travis asked.

"Because even with the good drugs, I can only sleep for so long," Brent replied. "And if anything was going to knock me out, it would be research. But it hasn't yet."

"I'm guessing you found something?"

Brent wiped a hand across his eyes. He was tired, which was to be expected. But it was "body tired" and not "brain tired," which meant that even if he lay down, his mind would keep going, and sleep would remain out of reach.

"Mark sent me a list of dead hunters that he hadn't had a chance to look into. A few of them were monster deaths, noted as 'attack by wild animal' in the official report. But the rest were mundane— hunting accidents, car wrecks, fell down a ravine, and a couple of self-inflicted gunshot wounds," Brent told him.

"All of which would be pretty normal if you didn't know they were hunters and if they hadn't all happened in the last two months," Brent concluded. "And while I was poking around, I found a couple of names I recognize from CHARON."

"Not sure that tells us anything new, but it helps to confirm the theory," Travis agreed.

"Yeah, well, wait till you hear the rest." Brent caught him up on the rest of Mark's comments, as well as what he was able to get from Shane about CHARON.

"That's not good." Travis's harried sigh told Brent that his partner wasn't surprised, but had held out a shred of hope that he might be wrong. "And it's more than I'd get if I called Father Liam or anyone else in Sinistram. But I think we go with our theory about them being behind everything until something proves us wrong. I just wish we could figure out the bigger plan."

Brent knew that just thinking about making contact with Father Liam was enough to trigger Travis, so he appreciated the sacrifice implicit in the offer.

"I don't think there's any point in making us a bigger target to

Sinistram than we already are," Brent replied. "I can almost under-stand—from their perspective—getting the amateur hunters out of the way. Although the risks we take are ones they don't have to, so we're valuable at least as cannon fodder."

"But regardless of how the causes of death were recorded, more monster sightings and hostile ghost reports mean that regular people outside the hunting community are noticing," Travis pointed out. "That stokes fear, and people react badly when they're afraid. Hence the first rule of Fight Club."

"Don't talk about it," Brent replied automatically. "Sooner or later, people are going to start talking."

"They already are." Travis recounted stories that several of the residents at St. Dismas had shared about more monsters on the streets, more homeless people disappearing, and evidence that the creatures were responsible. "Apparently there's a whole new cottage industry selling amulets and reading omens. Everyone's on edge."

"It's almost like part of their plan is to create the fear among regular people, and make the monsters more vulnerable as well as the hunters," Brent mused. "Maybe we shouldn't be looking for logic. Is it possible that someone just wants to see it all burn?"

"Wow, remind me not to give you the good drugs anymore," Travis responded. "Gloomy much?" He paused, and Brent knew Travis was taking a moment to seriously consider the question.

"The Church has a definite 'no one gets out alive' slant on the best of days," Travis replied. "And that's the Catholics—not counting the Protestant groups that believe in the 'End Times' and a final Apocalypse—capital 'A.' I've never been attracted to any of those theories because when you cut through the drama, destroying every-thing didn't make sense."

"That's because you're not a fanatic," Brent pointed out. "I could be totally off base. I hope I am. But when logical reasons don't pan out, you start looking at plausibly crazy."

"I hadn't thought to go in that direction, but I can put out some feelers. That would go along with all the talk of signs and portents,"

Travis replied. "In the meantime, get some rest. We've got a haunted circus wreck to handle."

"I feel a nap coming on," Brent replied, only partially in jest. "Let me know if you find out anything."

"You'll be the first person I call," Travis promised before he ended the call.

Brent stretched, finished his cup of coffee, and ate a couple of cookies before he returned to his computer. He wasn't ready to sleep yet, and he wanted to run down some possibilities while they were still fresh in his mind.

He dug a card out of his wallet, one that he had gathered when they had gone to the Steam and Gas show with Mark. Ed Finley owned the portable calliope, and Brent remembered him saying that it had been used in a circus long ago.

Finley picked up on the third ring. "Hello?" he answered cautiously, probably suspicious of an unfamiliar number.

"Mr. Finley, I met you at the Steam and Gas show when my friend and I were there with Mark Wojcik," Brent spoke quickly before Finley hung up. "You gave me your card. I thought of a couple of questions, if this isn't a bad time."

Finley laughed. "I'm retired, so unless I'm napping, there's not much going on. What's on your mind?"

"Did you ever hear of the Walter Brothers Circus?"

Finley was quiet for a moment. "Yes. Terrible thing that happened. But that was a long time ago. Why's a young guy like you interested?"

"Do you believe in circus hauntings?" Brent figured he'd just dive in.

This time, there was a longer pause. "Anyone who knows much about the circus believes in the ghosts," Finley replied. "Circuses were big operations—lots of people, wild animals, props, tents, railcars. Plenty of things could go wrong—and they did.

"Performers got hurt, animals got sick, tents caught on fire, and sometimes trains wrecked," he went on. "For all the 'show must go on' theatrics, there was a lot of hardship, even on a good day. The only one who ever got rich on a circus was P.T. Barnum. The smaller circuses squeaked by, barely making expenses. Performers didn't earn much, but most of them fit in better with circus folks than with civilians, so they stayed and made do."

Brent had read enough history and lore last night when sleep was scarce to validate Finley's less-than-glamorous description. Running away with the circus definitely wasn't all it was cracked up to be.

"Was there anything unusual about the Walter Brothers's accident?"

"It was a bad night," Finley said. "Rain, fog, and a winding stretch of track that had more than its share of wrecks. Circus cars weren't always new or in the best shape, although the good outfits tried to be safe. The reports chalked it up to wet rails, going too fast, and bad luck."

"What do you think?"

The question hung there for a moment. "I think that people look for explanations, and when they can't find one that suits them, they make them up," Finley said. "The Walter Brothers outfit was small potatoes, playing the second-tier cities. They weren't competing for the big arenas, so they weren't a threat to other operations."

The explanation was good, as far as it went. But Brent's intuition told him to keep digging.

"Did circuses have witches?" Brent remembered the mine magic and took a guess.

"Not that they admitted, but many did," Finley replied. "Circus people are particularly superstitious, and a little magic took some control back, put it in their own hands. Lots of folks wore amulets or had little shrines in their tents to protect themselves. Tattoos weren't as acceptable back in the day as they are now, but 'lifers,' performers who were with the circus for their whole careers, usually had a protective mark somewhere no one could see."

He paused. "I always figured the magic helped, but it couldn't keep away everything bad. The incident that destroyed the Walter

Brothers's show wasn't unusual as a wreck, only that it involved lions and tigers."

"Some of the performers died at the scene, didn't they?" Brent asked, confirming what he had found online.

"So did a few of the animals. People told stories that the lions had gotten loose and ate someone, but that's a bunch of hooey," Finley said. "I've never found any official or eyewitness accounts that back that up."

"Was the circus unlucky?"

"I guess that's in the eye of the beholder, but there were rumors at the time," Finley replied. "One of the survivors told the police the train had been hexed. There had been some accidents at the last show—a trapeze artist fell, and one of the fire show performers got burned. They closed up a day or two early because turnout wasn't good. I guess that could feel unlucky. And before you ask, my calliope isn't from Walter Brothers."

"Glad to hear it."

"Why are you interested in something that happened a hundred years ago?" Finley asked.

"Because we're getting reports of strange things happening near the accident site, and people have gotten hurt," Brent replied. "Whether it's ghosts, dark magic, or bad people, we need to make it stop."

"That's what you and your friend do? Hunt ghosts like on TV?" Finley asked.

"Yes, but it's not nearly as glamorous," Brent replied. "We just try to keep people from getting hurt and send the spirits on to rest."

"Huh. Just when you think you've heard everything," Finley said. "I don't know anything else about the Walter Brothers Circus, but if you haven't found it already, there's a pretty comprehensive website that has a collection of old timers' stories and photos. I haven't been out there in a while, but as I remember it, they had a nice collection about the Walter show." He gave Brent the web address.

"Thank you for your help," Brent said. "This has been great information."

Finley didn't rush to end the call, and Brent paid attention to his instincts that said the man had more to say.

"There's another legend connected to the Walter Brothers's wreck," Finley offered after a pause. "Anyone ever tell you about Eagle Eye Ike?"

Brent shook his head. "That's a new one. What's the story?"

"I don't know much, but back in the 1850s, there was a guy named Ike who was the grandson of runaway slaves. He was a farmer, and in his spare time, he hunted ghosts. Folks called him Eagle Eye Ike because he was a dead shot."

"He hunted ghosts?" Brent echoed, intrigued.

"Yep. Some folks thought he was crazy. Others whispered about Voodoo or some such. But when something they couldn't explain came around in the middle of the night, they'd send word and Ike would come and banish the ghost."

Brent knew that ghost hunters had been around throughout history, but at the same time, thanks to television, the idea felt oddly modern.

"Was he a witch?"

"No idea. By all accounts, he was a God-fearing church-goer. But according to the stories, when people got a fright and the priests and ministers didn't know what to do, Ike took up his shotgun and did what needed done."

"The circus wreck didn't happen until the 1890s." Brent frowned as he did the mental math. "Ike would have been really old to show up afterward and banish ghosts."

Finley chuckled. "By then, he was a ghost himself, still putting an end to harmful spirits and chasing off monsters. Lots of folks swore that it was the ghost of Eagle Eye Ike who chased away their haunts. Guess he thought the afterlife was too boring."

"That's quite a story." Brent knew he would be digging for resources as soon as the call ended.

"Didn't say I believe it, but you're likely to hear it from someone, if you don't run into Ike himself," Finley replied.

"One last question," Brent said. "Do you keep in touch with any of the smaller modern circuses? And if you do...any chance you know someone who might know a circus witch?"

Finley was quiet for a few moments, and Brent figured the man was deciding how far to trust him.

"Circus people are a special breed," he finally said. "Plenty superstitious. They're tight with their show family and suspicious of everyone else. With good reason. Outsiders might like the entertainment, but they often look askance at nomads who don't observe all the social conventions."

Brent heard the crinkle of a cigarette package and the flick of a lighter. "Got something to write down the number?" Finley asked.

Brent took down the digits on his phone and entered it as a contact. "You have a name for me?"

"Everyone calls her Helene," Finley said. "Probably not her real name, but when you go by it for long enough, that hardly matters. She's a tough bird, but if she likes you, she might tell you what you want to know. Left the circus and quit traveling a few years ago. Now she does blessings on shows that come to the area and is an elder for a community of retired circus folks that put down roots near here. They keep a low profile, and the locals leave them alone." Finley paused. "I'm trusting you not to fuck this up."

"I won't," Brent promised. "Thank you."

"Look, I don't know whether ghostbusters are for real, but if you are, I hope you can take care of whatever's causing the problem," Finley said. "Good luck."

The call ended, and Brent stared at his phone in silence for a few minutes, processing what Finley told him.

When he looked up, Danny was watching him with an accusing glare that Brent easily translated as an accusation of nearly ending up as a ghost.

"You saw?" Brent took comfort speaking aloud to Danny.

Danny nodded. He gave Brent a pointed glare, and Brent knew his brother thought he had taken too big a risk.

Brent sighed. "The situation got out of hand."

Danny cocked his head the way he always used to when he caught Brent in a falsehood, and the simple gesture flooded Brent's heart with feelings.

"Guilty." Brent held up a hand in appeasement. "We thought we had it covered and we didn't."

Danny frowned, and Brent knew the ghost wanted more information. Danny had always been intuitive, easily reading Brent and calling his bluff.

"Something's supercharging monsters and killing hunters," Brent replied. "I want to stop the deaths and not end up on the victim list. Hear anything about that?"

Danny shook his head.

"I used to think that ghosts somehow knew everything, like mind-readers," Brent said. "I guess not. I suppose there isn't a Grand Central Ghost Station where all the newly dead get welcomed to the afterlife for you to check out the new arrivals and look for dead hunters."

This time, Danny rolled his eyes. Then he gave Brent a look and pointed at him. Brent never had trouble knowing what was on Danny's mind, even long before he died. That hadn't changed.

"I never meant to worry you," Brent replied. "Sorry about that. Right now, we've got lots of suspicions, but not enough solid leads. And I can't shake the idea that it's all much bigger than just offing a few hunters."

He didn't need to hear Danny to guess what his brother would say, making him promise to trust his gut and reminding him that Danny didn't want Brent to cross over to him anytime soon.

Danny's ghost was fading, and Brent knew his brother couldn't keep the connection open for long.

"Thanks, kid. I miss you."

Danny faded out of view, but Brent imagined him saying, *"Kick it in the ass."*

Brent felt a mix of comfort and sadness after a visit from Danny, and being able to see his brother without help was fairly new. When Danny's spirit sacrificed himself to save others, he regained the ability to return to Brent slowly. Despite their bond, it wasn't nearly the same as having Danny with him in the flesh.

To break the mood, Brent got up and poured himself a fresh cup of coffee. He checked the dressings on his wounds, took the antibiotic and pain medicine Matthew had given him, and grabbed a box of crackers. He munched as he stared out the window, thinking of ghostly tigers and a hunter who kept watch even after death.

Armed with hot coffee, Brent looked for stories about Eagle Eye Ike. Now that he knew what to search for, his results lit up. Paranormal chat boards were full of supposed sightings. Sites catering to paranormal investigators and people who explored abandoned places shared stories that they swore happened to them.

Brent was used to trying to parse urban legend from real supernatural situations. Most of the Eagle Eye Ike stories had a ring of truth. They weren't sensational, and they didn't make Ike out to be a superhero. Other than the advantage of not being able to be killed because he was already dead, the tales recounted a ghostly man who showed up to rescue people from harmful ghosts armed with an old-fashioned shotgun.

Brent grabbed a map and started to mark where Ike had been spotted. While the majority of the incidents had been north and east of Pittsburgh, the Walter Circus case was at the western edge of where Ike had been sighted.

His phone rang, and Brent had been concentrating so hard that he jumped. "Travis," he greeted, "ever hear stories about Eagle Eye Ike?"

"Wasn't he a ghost hunter, back in the day?" Travis sounded confused at the unexpected question. Brent felt vaguely disappointed not to be the first to share the story.

"I talked to the guy who owned the calliope at the steam show, and he said to watch for Ike if we went to chase away the ghosts at the circus wreck site," Brent said.

"Makes me wonder why there's still a haunting, if it's in his territory," Travis said.

Brent was grateful his partner didn't doubt the story. "Maybe there are too many ghosts for a hunter who's a ghost himself. Or maybe he can only do so much as a spirit, and he's kept the haunting from being more dangerous, but he doesn't have the mojo to stop it altogether."

"Interesting theory," Travis allowed. "As long as he doesn't get in our way, I won't turn down help, living or dead."

CHAPTER FIVE

"YOU'RE SUPPOSED TO BE RESTING," Travis protested when Brent called to sell him on the idea of going to New Castle to interview Helene.

"She's a circus witch," Brent countered. "And she might be able to give us some tips—or spells—to help set the Walter Brothers's ghosts to rest."

"Yeah, but—"

"Matthew cleared me to drive," Brent said. "But I'm asking you to drive so I don't have to. That counts as resting."

Travis sighed, knowing when it wasn't worth arguing. "Okay, but if it takes longer for you to feel better, don't blame me."

"Helene didn't seem surprised when I called her," Brent said.

"Ya' think Finley warned her, or is she psychic?"

"Damned if I know, but she invited us to come talk and gave me her address," Brent replied. "Either she's the real deal or it's some kind of trap."

Travis frowned. "Unless Finley was in on it somehow, I can't figure how it could be a trap. Not like we're the trusting sort, regardless."

"Guess you're right."

Brent typed the address into his phone for directions, and they headed out. "Did you ever hear of a circus town outside of New Castle?"

"Can't say I did, not that I ever looked for it," Travis replied. "What is a circus town, anyhow?"

Brent grinned, and Travis knew his partner had been using his search engine talents to do a deep dive.

"Circuses were top-tier entertainment back in the late 1800s. Some of the big names from then are still around now, like Ringling Brothers, but dozens of smaller companies spent the good weather months traveling to towns near railroad lines and putting on a weekend show," Brent told him.

"They were often called 'ten-cent shows' because that's all they charged for a full day of trapeze artists, clowns, trained dogs and horses, live music, snake handlers, and everything from dramatic readings to people who used their physical oddities to make a living as a performer," Brent said.

"And one of those shows was based in New Castle?"

Brent nodded. "The Hurlburt and Hunting Circus lasted into the early part of the 1900s. In the off-season, the performers needed somewhere to live, train, and house their animals. They had a little enclave on the outskirts of New Castle. They didn't bother anyone, and the locals apparently didn't mind them being there. When people retired, they stayed and helped run the circus town."

"This new friend of yours has to be way too young to remember those days, unless she's a ghost," Travis said.

"Finley says she's very much alive. The Hunting Circus closed, but the enclave remained, and so did its reputation as a safe place for circus folks. Most people have forgotten all about that piece of local history, and I think that suits the community residents just fine," Brent told him.

"So we need to be careful about not blowing their cover."

"I make it a habit not to annoy people who have trained snakes for a living," Brent said with a deadpan expression.

The GPS took them around New Castle to what looked like a small town swallowed by the modern developments around it. "Welcome to Gibbstown," a sign said.

A tidy community of houses and shops lined the road and stretched a few blocks on either side. Many of the houses were Victorians, while others dated from across the last century. A café, general store, bakery, and a couple of other well-maintained businesses looked like they were doing okay.

"Looks pretty ordinary," Travis observed.

"You were expecting circus tents?" Brent joked. "Pet tigers in the backyard?"

Travis shrugged. "Didn't know what to expect."

They parked at the curb near their destination, and Brent looked up at the sign that hung above the door. "'Fortune Coffee.' Guess this is the right place."

Inside, the warmly lit, cozy interior had fanciful paintings of dogs and cats on the walls. The air smelled of roasting beans and fresh baked goods. Not a single detail referenced the circus or traveling shows.

They walked to the counter and ordered two drinks. "I'm looking for Helene," Brent told the woman at the register. "I called this morning. I'm Brent, and this is Travis."

She nodded. "Figured that. I know everyone in town. I'm Helene."

Helene looked to be in her late forties or early fifties, a tall, spare woman with dark hair shot through with gray pulled back in a ponytail. Rolled-up sleeves revealed sinewy arms and strong hands. An apron over a T-shirt and jeans read, "Good Fortune Starts Here."

"Take the back table. I'll be over as soon as Jane can cover for me." Helene called to a woman working in the back as they ambled over to their seats, and followed a few minutes later.

"So...tell me what you want to know, and I'll see if I can help."

"We want to know about circus witches, and Finley said you might have some history on the topic," Brent said.

Helene laughed. "Some history? Yeah, I guess you could say that." She closed her eyes for a moment, concentrating. When she opened them, she looked at both men differently, as if she could see through them. "You lay spirits to rest and stop monsters." It wasn't a question.

"We help them move on and keep them from hurting the living," Travis replied.

"There's a place where a circus train wrecked many years ago—people and animals died," Brent replied. "It was dormant for a long time, but now the ghosts are acting up, causing danger. We want to help them pass over and keep people from getting hurt. I was hoping you might know something that would help."

They weren't usually quite so plain-spoken, but something about Helene made Brent trust her and told him she would respect straight-forwardness.

She nodded. "I've heard many stories about the wreck and visited the site a few times. Unfortunately crashes like that weren't unknown in the circus world back then, but that particular one is among the worst. I'm not surprised the ghosts aren't settled."

"We think there may be a malicious third party riling up haunt-ings to draw out hunters and attack them," Travis replied, and both men waited to see her reaction.

Helene hesitated as if listening to a voice they could not hear. "There is truth to what you say. How did you think I could help?"

Brent gave an uncertain smile. "That's part of what we came here to figure out. We thought maybe you might have some additional insight since you were also part of the circus."

She chuckled. "When I traveled with the show, I was the fortune teller. Behind the scenes, I worked protective magic, helped the medics with healing, and kept away the dark things. Since I retired from the circuit, I still do all those things, but I sleep in my own bed every night, which is something I truly appreciate."

"Can you help us? Will you?" Travis asked.

Helene looked from Brent to Travis. "Before I give you my answer, I want to share a story I heard about the wreck soon after I came to Gibbstown. One of our oldest residents, Joe McLaughlin, was a rigger with several shows. He came from a circus family, going back generations. One of his ancestors had been with the Walter Brothers and survived the crash."

She paused and took another sip of tea. "Joe said that the story that came down through the family held that there was a supernatural cause to the wreck. He didn't know all the details—old stories like that always leave a lot out—but the piece that endured and that his ancestor apparently swore on a Bible was true was that vampires had something to do with it."

"Vampires?" Brent hadn't anticipated that revelation.

Helene nodded. "Joe certainly believed the story to be true, and apparently so did his family members. Figured you should know."

"Thank you," Travis replied. "Here's hoping none of them show up when we go to deal with the restless ghosts, but we'll take precautions."

"Which brings us back to the beginning," Brent added. "Is there anything you can tell us about the magic to help us with the spirits?"

Helene gave an enigmatic smile. "I can do better than that. I'll go with you. Circus folks stick together."

Travis felt a weight he didn't know he carried slip from his shoulders. He wasn't sure why he felt so relieved to have the witch's help, but it was like a piece of a puzzle slotting into place, one he hadn't realized had been missing.

"Thank you." Brent sounded as relieved as Travis. "I didn't think we could ask you for that, but I believe it will make a difference."

"So do I," Helene said, "although my sources haven't explained why. I've been out to the wreck site a few times over the years. When it was closer to living memory, people wanted to lay a wreath on the anniversary of the crash. The ghosts never bothered us, but even then, I knew they hadn't made their peace and moved on. When spirits linger too long, someone or something is going to rile them up and cause trouble eventually. I consider this to be part of the healing I do in the community."

They spent the next half hour making plans and agreed to meet up once Brent had been cleared for action by Matthew.

Helene gave Brent a look that seemed to see down to his bones. "You've been injured recently by something supernatural. It's left a mark on you."

"I got hurt on a hunt," Brent replied.

Helene shook her head. "I know demon energy when I sense it. On top of your new injury."

Ben didn't like to remember his run-in with Mavet in Mosul, or his brushes with demons since then. He had suspected that something attracted them, but hearing confirmation didn't help his mood.

Helene ran a hand just above the surface of Brent's arm and leg where the gnome had clawed him, and her lips moved silently as she concentrated.

"Gnomes are nasty business," Helene said, even though neither man had mentioned Brent's attacker. "Supernatural injuries often fester. Yours is clean and healing well. I added a little something to help things along," she added with a smile.

"Thank you." Brent's features looked less pinched, telling Travis that the healing had been effective.

"Call me when you're ready to go," Helene told them as they took their leave. "I'll keep my calendar open over the next couple of days."

CHAPTER SIX

TWO DAYS LATER, after winning Matthew's grudging clearance, Brent and Travis headed toward the site of the Walter Brothers's wreck. Helene had agreed to meet them there.

Brent fidgeted on the drive to the site of the circus train crash.

"Penny for your thoughts," Travis prompted. After all the ghosts he and Brent had sent packing, the fairly routine banishment didn't seem like it should set his partner on edge.

Brent didn't seem surprised that Travis had picked up on his jitters, since he vibrated with nervous energy. "I'm edgier than usual, and I'm not sure why."

Travis shrugged. "Listen to your intuition. Is it worried that we don't know enough about the hunt, or something else?"

Brent took a deep breath and paused as if silently asking himself that question. "I'm wondering what riled up the circus train ghosts and whether it's tied into whoever is trying to kill hunters."

"You think it's a setup?"

"Could be," Brent replied. "Didn't you question it, coming up now after all this time?"

"Yeah. I think we need to be extra careful," Travis said. "Maybe get some of the friendly ghosts to scout the area and see if there's someone else around."

"It's daylight, so that should keep the vampires away, if they're involved," Brent noted. "Although I guess they could always send in their minions. Think Ike will show up?"

Travis snorted. "He hasn't bothered to so far, although I'll never turn down help."

Brent pulled up his case notes on his phone, even though Travis knew he had read them over multiple times. "The Walter Brothers circus wasn't a big outfit. Back then there were plenty of second-string shows that crisscrossed the country to entertain the smaller cities, like the one that was in New Castle."

"The train lost its brakes on a long hill, and there was a curve at the bottom," Travis recalled from his research. "Some of their cars were heavier than normal trains, which probably didn't help. The engine made it around the bend, but the other cars went off the tracks."

"Most of the performers survived," Brent noted, checking his phone. "Unfortunately, a lot of the horses and exotic animals were killed or injured. A Bengal tiger got loose and scared a lady who was milking her cows. She ran away, and the tiger killed the cows."

"That's actually documented," Travis replied, shaking his head. "But people claimed to see parrots and lions and even a few kangaroos for years afterward."

"Not too many native kangaroos in this part of Pennsylvania," Brent agreed with a chuckle, then sobered as he looked back at his notes. "The train's brakeman died in the wreck, and the coal tenders, along with some of the circus people. The people were buried in the closest town cemetery, and the animals were buried in a pit dug near the wreck site."

"Yeah, I read that. Which makes me wonder about the haunting. If the people were properly buried on sacred ground, then who are the ghosts?" Travis asked.

"Most of the reports talk about people seeing horses and zoo-type animals, like lions and bears," Brent replied. "Although there have also been stories about a headless man in a train-worker's jumpsuit walking the old rail line at night with a lantern. The legends say he'll kill anyone he catches."

"Yeah, but the records don't say anyone was decapitated," Travis pointed out. "The brakeman was crushed, and the other train crew who died were burned by the boiler and coal fire. The circus performers were thrown from the car and died from the impact."

Travis drummed his fingers against the steering wheel. "For a lot of crashes, I'd guess that the ghosts were restless being buried so far from home. But for the performers, the circus was their home. They moved around all the time. The train belonged to the circus, so I'd guess the same was true for the crewmen."

"Helene said some of the survivors came back every year for decades to commemorate the wreck," Brent said. "I found an article about it. In the first couple of years, they even had elephants lay a wreath at the marker by the accident site."

"That must have kept the locals entertained." Travis chuckled. "If I read the account right, the railroad re-routed a section of the track to flatten out the hill and make the curve less sharp. They never admitted any fault for the wreck, but since they had to fix the track anyhow, I guess they decided it was a problem waiting to happen again the way it was."

"About those commemorations," Brent said. "From what I could find, the ghost sightings started after the ceremonies ended. Maybe the ghosts got angry that people stopped coming, but the story faded, and the survivors got old and died."

"Wouldn't be the first time ghosts didn't want to be forgotten. I also wonder whether or not there were items left behind from the wreck that tether the ghosts to the area," Travis mused.

"I can see things being overlooked in the original cleanup," Brent replied, "but in all the years afterward, I'd think curiosity-seekers would have found anything of note."

"We've seen it before, anchors don't have to be large," Travis said.

"Bits of metal, something from the circus itself…ghosts are bound to the oddest things. And the accounts from the time say that the towns-folk who came out to see what happened walked away with souvenirs of the wreck, any of which could be a 'ghost beacon.'"

"The sightings have become more frequent in the last few months…not surprising considering the anniversary of the wreck is coming up," Brent pointed out. "No one's gotten hurt yet, but the interactions are worrisome.

"At first, people who were walking the trails said they heard a train whistle, then a crash, and the sounds of frightened horses," he continued. "Then a few months later, there were reports of glimpsing exotic animals in the woods, only there weren't any tracks or evidence of living creatures."

Travis nodded. "Then there were new reports of ghost horses running across nearby roads, and a woman in white wandering in the woods where the tracks used to be. And even though the railroad changed its route, the people I talked to said that there are crews that will do everything they can to avoid working that run, because they say it's bad luck."

"Even on the new route, there have been more accidents and fatalities than usual," Brent said. "Railroaders are superstitious, and it's already dangerous work. Once a route gets a reputation for being unlucky, the story sticks."

"And if someone, or *something*, is souping up monsters to draw out hunters and attack them, it sounds like perfect bait," Travis pointed out.

"That occurred to me."

"I didn't think we'd actually start hauling even more stuff to a ghost hunt, but here we are," Brent said as he and Travis unpacked the trunk of the Crown Victoria.

"We haven't usually needed to watch for human and ghostly dangers at the same time, or tigers," Travis pointed out.

Travis powered on the MEL meter, an instrument that scanned

for unusually cold spots, looking for where the circus haunts might be lurking.

"The ghosts of a couple of deer hunters and hikers are here," Travis said. "I asked them to help us keep an eye out for intruders."

"Getting anything from the circus ghosts?" Brent asked.

"I'm picking up energy, but not sentience." Travis spoke slowly as if he needed to think through his response. "Not real close, but definitely along the old rail line. I don't know whether they haven't noticed us yet, don't care, or just hope we'll go away."

"Or we haven't crossed into their territory," Brent said. Ghosts could be oddly particular about such things.

They heard a car approaching and shifted their stance to block the newcomer's view of their trunk, then relaxed as they recognized the driver.

Helene pulled in and parked. "Good morning," she greeted as she joined them. "Ready to meet some ghosts?" She carried a black crocheted bag and wore charms Travis recognized as powerful protection symbols.

They left the cars behind and hiked the rest of the way, with Brent watching for cold-spot signals while Travis and Helene kept an eye out for manifestations.

Travis glimpsed shadowy forms in the distance as the sensor pinged. The ghosts knew they were there and were waking up.

"They're trying to figure out why we've come," Helene said quietly. "The ghosts are in a lot of turmoil. That's new. Something's gotten them riled up."

The closer they got to the site of the wreck, the stronger Travis felt the ghostly presence and the uncomfortable itch of dark power. "I agree. Could someone have planted a talisman or worked magic to make the ghosts angry?"

She closed her eyes to focus. Brent and Travis stayed close, protecting her and scanning the tree line for threats.

"Definitely dark magic," she said a moment later as she opened her eyes and looked around them. "Powerful, but fairly new. Not the kind of spell a novice witch could work."

Travis and Brent exchanged a glance. *That means we've got a strong rogue mage, or the Sinistram is up to something.*

"If you and Travis work together, can you break it?" Brent asked. "I'll keep watch."

Helene considered for a moment. "I think we stand a chance. Just remember, the ghosts never really left this place. They just went to sleep for a while. Whatever tethered them is still providing an anchor."

Brent put his hands on his hips and turned in a circle, trying to see the land the way it had appeared in the old photographs of the train wreck.

"How do you find their anchor after a hundred years?" Brent mused. "Souvenir hunters and history buffs have been over the area time and again, and they probably carried off anything portable."

Travis stood in a spot where he could still make out the depression from the long-ago rails. "Then we look for something they couldn't carry off."

"The reports said that the rails were taken up; those that weren't were twisted and bent from the crash. Cleanup crews cleared the wrecked circus cars and hauled away the passenger cars," Brent reported.

"I imagine the cleanup was rushed, as usual," Helene replied. "Things get left behind."

They spread out, staying in sight of one another, walking the stretch of the old railroad line where the crash had occurred. Before long, Brent called to the others from where he stood not far inside the line of trees.

"They didn't bother clearing all the rail once the line went into the forest." Travis pointed to the ground where he had kicked away dirt and exposed a rusted section of metal.

"You can still see where the tracks went." Brent directed their attention to a narrow but unnaturally straight gap. Saplings had grown and grass covered the rails, but the older trees clearly marked the corridor.

"Since they rerouted the line, no one needed this section anymore," Travis replied. "It might even still belong to the railroad. No one's been in a hurry to do anything else with it."

"Being haunted might have something to do with that," Helene remarked in a dry tone.

Brent kicked at the ground, revealing wooden crossties between the rails. "Now it makes sense." He invited the others for a closer look. "I couldn't figure out how the rails themselves could be an anchor, because they're steel, which has a lot of iron in it, and ghosts don't like iron. But they also left the wooden crossties, so I guess that was enough."

Helene closed her eyes and concentrated. "The ghosts are still attached to the area. That's nothing new. But they're angry. I'd almost say in pain, if that were possible. That's different. And I don't think it's natural."

She began walking along the old rails, intent on the ground. "Take a section and look for something new, something not natural that might have been planted to get the ghosts in an uproar."

Helene headed away from them. Brent went the other way, while Travis ran ahead to check a section farther down the way.

Brent paid close attention, looking for anywhere the ground looked freshly disturbed. After unearthing a few caches of nuts and pinecones buried by animals, he kicked at a mound and then bent down for a closer look. "Hey, what do you make of this?"

Travis and Helene joined him as Brent gingerly poked at the dirt with a stick to reveal a talisman that looked like it had been made from twigs and sinew.

"Don't touch it," Helene warned. "It's dark magic. Might not be the only thing riling up the ghosts, but I'm sure it's part of the problem."

Brent withdrew a small flask of lighter fluid and a lighter. "Would this help?"

"If you can burn it without setting the woods on fire," she replied. "And be ready, there's no telling how the ghosts will respond."

"Although we probably shouldn't burn it until we do the incantation," Travis warned.

Deep in the woods, Travis thought he heard the rumble of a lion or a tiger. He didn't want to find out how much damage a ghostly big cat could cause. "On your six," Helene warned, and Travis turned as several gray ghosts emerged from the trees. They wore regular clothes for their time periods, not circus garb.

"Behind you," Helene said, and Travis saw a ghost of a headless man in a conductor's uniform carrying a lantern.

A ghostly tiger came bounding from the forest. Travis unloaded his shotgun filled with salt rounds, and it disappeared, only to be replaced by a spectral lion.

The temperature dropped, and Travis could see his breath mist. At least a dozen human ghosts shimmered into sight, along with a large bear and another tiger. Their clothing matched the era of the circus wreck, and Travis guessed their spirits had not followed their remains to burial. Travis had no intention of letting them get too close.

"Watch out!" Brent warned. "They're strong enough, even I can see some of them."

Helene began to chant, but she kept her eyes open and tossed handfuls of salt at any ghosts that came too close.

The bear circled to the right while the tiger went left, two apex predators sizing up their prey, even after death. The angry circus ghosts moved in, cutting off escape. In their recent fights, the human ghosts had been on his side, but these spirits definitely looked hostile.

Brent cocked his shotgun and fired at the bear. It vanished, only to reappear seconds later, even closer. The other ghosts didn't slow their approach, and shooting the tiger didn't stop him.

Two of the ghosts wore acrobat costumes, advancing with theatrical handsprings and flips. Three others tossed knives back and forth, never missing. A blood-spattered clown would definitely figure in Travis's future nightmares, especially when he opened his crimson mouth and breathed out fire.

Brent fired again and again, trying to hold off the ghosts long enough for Helene and Travis to work their banishment. He backed away from the spirits, limited to how far he could retreat by the tiger and the bear who continued to circle them.

"Try to hold them back long enough for us to destroy the talisman," Travis shouted. That would sever the spirits' bond to the site of the wreck and stop the haunting.

Helene chanted louder. Travis added his voice to hers in the rite of banishment.

"Look!" Brent pointed to a new ghost who appeared nearly in the middle of the stand-off. He was tall and lanky with dark skin and workman's clothing from a century past. He held a knife in his left hand and a vodun cross in his right.

Eagle Eye Ike. He came, Travis thought.

Ike raised the cross and planted himself between the lion and the living. His mouth moved, but Travis couldn't hear Ike's words, although the ghosts recoiled.

More ghosts appeared along the old rail line, but these wore clothing from a variety of time periods, the spirits of people killed in accidents over the decades. They interposed themselves between the circus specters and the living people.

"Ike bought us time, and the new ghosts are holding back the dangerous spirits," Travis said. He didn't know how long their unexpected defenders could hold back the others. "Brent, now!"

"Fire in the hole!" Brent called out as he lit up the talisman. Flames leaped higher than they should have for the amount of fluid he used, hissing and popping, and Travis swore he heard screams.

The tiger roared, and its solid-looking apparition vanished. So did the lion and the vengeful performers. The protective ghosts were the last to go, remaining until the threat was gone as if they were unaffected by the burned talisman and left of their own accord. One of them tipped his fedora to them before winking out of sight.

That left Ike, who also seemed unaffected by the ritual.

"Thank you," Travis said to the ghost. Brent and Helene added their thanks as well. Ike just smiled, inclined his head in acknowledgment, and vanished.

Travis let out a breath. He looked to Helene and Brent. "Is everyone okay?"

Helene nodded. "A little drained. I was saying protective spells, and I also sent out a psychic call to Ike. I guess you could say that he and I are old friends. He's come to lend a hand on several occasions."

Travis turned in a slow circle, searching the area for any sign of remaining ghosts. "Do you think that will send the dangerous ghosts away for good?"

"Guess we wait and see." Helene replaced several ritual items into her bag. "It shouldn't affect the protector spirits. They choose to stay as guardians, like Ike. I hope we've sent the others on to find peace." They waited for half an hour, but nothing stirred. Travis and Brent walked Helene back to her car.

"Good working with you," she told them. "Call me if you need anything else. I'm happy to help. I don't control when Ike shows up, but he's often on board for a good cause."

Elated but tired, Travis and Brent headed back to Pittsburgh. By unspoken agreement, they kept the conversation light on the drive and during lunch at a diner they passed on the way.

Travis's phone rang as they got back into the Crown Vic after their meal. He frowned and swore under his breath.

"Trouble?" Brent asked.

"Sinistram," Travis replied. "Dominick here," he said as he answered the phone, using only his last name. He didn't bother with pleasantries, and his tone made it clear the contact wasn't welcome.

A cold chuckle on the other side fed Travis's anger, and he recognized the voice of Father Liam, his Sinistram mentor.

"Dominick. Still the same. Some things never change."

"What do you want?"

"I'm calling to warn you. The world is changing. The end is near. Return to the Sinistram and you'll be protected," Liam said.

"The world is always changing. Warn me about what? Protect me from whom?" Over the years, the Sinistram had tried and failed to entice Travis to return to its authority. Time had just increased his conviction to remain free of their entanglements.

"We've been patient," Father Liam said, and his voice hardened. "That time is over. Return or face the consequences."

"Fuck you." Travis ended the call before Liam could reply. Only then did he realize that his hand shook as he held the phone. Just the sound of Father Liam's voice knotted Travis's stomach.

"That didn't sound good," Brent observed. "Do you need a break? I can drive."

"I'll actually process better if I'm driving," Travis replied. "I'll just stew if I'm the passenger."

"Suit yourself. The offer stands."

Travis headed toward home. Neither man spoke for a while. Brent had to notice that Travis opted for back roads rather than the highway, but he didn't mention it.

"Dammit," Travis said after a long pause. "This is so like them, dangling imminent hellfire and damnation, and all you have to do to be saved is fall in line and not ask questions."

"The Library Keepers harass you, but it's been a while since you've gotten a call from the Mothership, hasn't it?" Brent asked.

"Yeah, not that I missed them. I was hoping they finally caught the hint and gave up. Should have known better." He knew Brent could hear the anger and bitterness in his voice.

"Unless Father Liam has a call list of prodigal priests and just happened to get to your name today, there's got to be a reason why he's making another effort now," Brent said, employing the skills that made him such a good detective. "So...what's changed?"

"As far as we know, just the angry ghosts and people killing hunters," Travis replied. "I don't follow insider Church politics, so if there's a battle for the next Sinistram Cardinal position, I don't know anything about it."

Brent shook his head. "If there were, Liam wouldn't call you about it. There's nothing you could do to change the course. But what if it does have something to do with whatever's hunting the hunters and provoking the ghosts and monsters? What did he mean 'the end is coming'? Is there any way, however wildly unlikely, that the trouble we've been investigating has some link back to the Sinistram?"

Travis bit back an automatic negative and forced himself to think. "The Sinistram has always considered itself to be better than run-of-the-mill hunters because they're priests and steeped in occult lore and have some sort of paranormal abilities."

No matter that the group remained conflicted over whether those abilities were God-given or sinful, they used their magic to stop large supernatural dangers. Travis also suspected that the priests weren't above using their talents to influence decision-makers and affect the course of events to shape the outcome.

"They might not like the regular hunters, but there are too many angry ghosts and hungry monsters for the Sinistram to take them all on," Brent said. "These situations pop up all over the country and the world. There aren't enough priests anywhere to take care of all of them, even if they quit doing weddings, christenings, and funerals."

"We've got to be missing something," Travis fretted. "I guess that if no one protected people from ghosts and monsters, maybe people would be frightened into going back to church to save their souls, but that seems like a long shot."

"They'd probably drink the liquor stores dry first," Brent replied. "You can always make a deathbed confession, but getting a shot of whiskey in your last moments isn't as easy."

"Heathen." Travis managed to joke despite the situation.

"Proudly."

"I'm trying to think through all our contacts to see if anyone might have an inside track on what's going on, and no one is coming to mind." Travis knew he sounded as tired as he felt.

"We're pretty well connected to the supernatural world, but not so much to the Vatican," Brent said. "What about Father Anne?"

"She's Episcopalian. So probably not." Travis paused. "And before you ask, Father Pavel, Father Ryan, and Father Leo aren't Sinistram, just regular priests. I don't want to drag them into this. They won't hear the gossip, and I won't make them targets."

"Fair enough," Brent agreed.

"You know, the bruhaha with Sinistram and the whole issue with hunters being hunted might be completely unrelated," Travis said.

Brent snorted. "When is anything in our lives simple like that?"

"As for his talk about 'the end,' that's always been part of Sinistram lore," Travis said. "They actually believe there will be an apocalypse that will scour the world and burn it clean. Weirdly enough, they seem to look forward to it, although they've been watching for signs and omens since the Order was founded. So far, we're all still here."

They spent the rest of the drive talking about anything except priests and paranormal problems. It was after dark when he pulled up to Brent's house.

"Hey, did you see that?" Brent craned his neck to look at the night sky through the windshield.

"See what?"

"Falling stars," Brent said, pointing. "My grandmother always told me to make a wish."

Travis crossed himself. "Mine told me to say a prayer against evil. I think I like your grandma better."

Brent reached for the car door.

"Wait." Travis put a hand on Brent's arm. "Something's wrong."

Brent gave him a sharp look. "Wrong, how?"

Before Travis could answer, a body landed on the hood and windshield with a thud, and a young, blond man flashed a fanged smile at them.

"Like that." Travis slammed the Crown Vic into reverse, but the vampire managed to hang on.

"Brace yourself," Travis warned, going as fast in reverse as he dared on the side street. He swerved from side to side, hoping to dislodge the attacker, who held on despite everything.

"Holy shit." Brent grabbed the armrest and planted his feet wide, ready for a crash.

Travis found an empty parking lot and floored it, steering into tight circles that would have broken a human's grip. Nothing worked to shake their attacker.

Travis couldn't imagine how it must look to bystanders, and he didn't have time to worry about it.

"You're in the way," the vamp shouted through the windshield. "I was sent with a message. Back off."

"Who sent you?" Brent shouted as Travis raced down side streets not intended for high speeds.

"God works in mysterious ways." The vampire had a glint in his eyes like he was on a drugged blood high, and his predicament didn't seem to worry him.

"Here goes nothing." Travis sent them down Canton Avenue, the steepest street not just in Pittsburgh but in the entire United States, hoping gravity and speed would dislodge their unwelcome passenger. He swerved back and forth, glad it was one-way and that they were long after rush hour.

Travis steered to hit a pothole without reducing speed. The jolt loosened the vampire's grip, and the car cut hard to one side, sending him tumbling off. For good measure, Travis ran him over, then slammed into reverse and did it again, making sure to spin the tires. He didn't know if that would destroy the vampire, but it certainly wouldn't be pleasant.

"Did you just—" Brent stared in the rearview mirror to see the bloodied vampire stagger to his feet.

"Yeah." Travis expected to feel the vampire slam into them from behind at any second and was ready for another attack. When that didn't happen, he took a deep breath.

"Can't kill a dead man, but I guess he decided not to go for round two." Travis slowed the car and watched to make sure the cops hadn't noticed them.

"Or maybe he delivered his message and was done."

Travis slid a look toward Brent. "Meaning?"

"Sounds like he was sent. Who do we know who thinks they speak for God?"

"You think the Sinistram sent a *vampire* to warn us off?" Even as Trent said the words, something settled in his gut telling him it was true. "Why?"

Brent chewed his lip as he thought for a moment. Travis drove up and down streets randomly, making sure they had shaken their pursuer. "Who thinks even more highly of themselves than the Sinistram?" Brent said after a long pause.

"Vampires? Yeah, most of them are pretentious bastards with a few exceptions. But the Sinistram kills vampires."

Brent turned to look at him. "What if there was some sort of alliance between apex predators, as it were? A business deal. Stop killing ours and we'll stop killing yours."

The possibility made Travis's head spin. "That would be a big change. Huge. I can't imagine getting it past Cardinal Vasylyk. He hates anything paranormal. And certainly not past the Vatican."

"You've said many times that The Sinistram runs on lies and misdirection. How involved is the Cardinal in day-to-day affairs? Does he live in the US, or is he in Rome most of the time? It's not like the vampires would have to be inside headquarters." Brent ran with the possibilities.

"Let's say you're right." Travis still grappled with the idea. "It would be a huge mission shift for a truce."

"Maybe not just a truce," Brent said. "Vampires are old. They know things. Some of them were witches and alchemists before being turned. Plenty of them gained fortunes and exerted political power over people they've bought off or put into thrall. Money, inside knowledge, and power, exactly what the Sinistram lusts after."

Travis shuddered at the juxtaposition of "Sinistram" and "lust" since the leaders he met from the organization looked dour and cadaverous, far removed from the temptations of the flesh.

"Poor word choice?" Brent asked with a laugh, as if he guessed Travis's thoughts.

"Yeah." His mind whirred, looking for connections. "I keep going back to how rough they were on me because of my abilities, even though they use the same magic and mediumship. The Church has an unfortunate history of lying when it suits its purposes. So, although collaborating with vampires is a total mind-fuck, it's possible."

"Do you mind if I stay at St. Dismas again tonight?" Brent asked. "Just in case there's another vamp back at mine."

"Did you notice that's where I'm heading? I kinda figured that."

"Thanks." Brent sounded rattled, and his leg jittered, a sure tell.

"You want to stop somewhere for a drink? No alcohol at St. Dismas, but you look like you could use one," Travis offered.

"Sure. Pick a place. Should be random enough that no one expects us."

Travis pulled up in front of a package store and waited in the car while Brent ran in and returned with a flask of Jack Daniels. He shook his head when Brent offered a nip.

"Can't. Driving. Might need to run over another vamp or two."

Brent's chuckle didn't reach his eyes. He knocked back a couple of long slugs and let out a satisfied breath. "That...helps."

"You don't have to drink the whole thing," Travis said. "You can leave it in the glove compartment. Just can't take it into the building."

Brent wasn't the only former soldier and monster hunter who had a complicated relationship with alcohol. Travis worried, but he didn't judge. The kind of trauma Brent survived losing Danny and his family to demons, only to encounter more demonic attacks on deployment, went far beyond what therapists and medications could temper.

Travis scanned for danger as he used voice-activation to call Jon.

"I'm heading your way. Brent's staying another night. We got jumped by a vampire at his house, but I ran over it. Need to go back in daylight and make sure there aren't any other surprises."

"Okaaaay." Jon drew the word out, but took the comment in stride. Travis figured that was a testimony to how weird their lives were.

"Just to be safe, figure we're on high alert," Travis told him. "Anyone who comes in has to pass the tests. No one goes out. Activate the wards. I'll shore them up when I get there. Make sure all the doors, windows, and vents are protected."

"Not my first rodeo," Jon assured him. "It's been a slow night, so that's good. How close are you?"

"About five minutes. As far as I can tell, we haven't been followed. Although if we're guessing right about who sent the vamps, they already know where I live," Travis replied.

"That's not reassuring at all," Jon said. "Are either of you hurt? Matthew's on standby."

"For once, we're okay. Although we'd have gotten a few more holes in us if that vampire hadn't been so eager." Travis didn't want to think about how things might have gone if the attacker had waited for him to drop Brent off and leave before revealing himself. Brent could take care of himself in a fight against monsters, but being ambushed and not having the right set of weapons could change the odds dramatically.

Travis let out a sigh of relief when St. Dismas came into view. Brent took another long pull from the flask, then obligingly stuffed it into the glove compartment. Travis pulled the car into his reserved spot, which was well-lit and protected by magic and wards. He glanced around but saw no one nearby.

"Let's go."

Brent grabbed his bag, and Travis locked the car. Jon was waiting for him at the door to usher them inside.

"Busy night?" he asked.

"You don't know the half of it." Travis still struggled with the attack and Sinistram's possible betrayal. "We'll fill you in tomorrow morning."

CHAPTER SEVEN

AFTER BREAKFAST, Brent and Travis holed up in the apartment at St. Dismas to make calls. Travis checked in with the loose network of people with minor supernatural abilities he called his "Night Vigil," and Brent called allies they had worked with on previous cases.

"Cassidy," Brent said when he rang Deadly Curiosities and its owner, Cassidy Kincaide answered. "Do you have a minute? Got a potentially world-ending question for you."

"Hello to you, too," Cassidy replied, not sounding perturbed at the apocalyptic potential. "What's up?"

Cassidy's antique and curio shop had been in her family for generations, and like her ancestors, her psychometry gave her the ability to read the history and magic of objects by touching them. She and her friends in Charleston, SC, protected the city from supernatural attacks and lent their expertise to other hunters and witches, including consulting on magic and lore.

"Has Sorren heard anything about a vampire conspiracy?" Brent asked. Sorren, a nearly 600-year-old vampire, was Cassidy's business partner and used his unique abilities as a guardian protecting mortals.

She chuckled. "You know they don't all know each other, right? I don't think there's an actual 'vampire network.'"

"Or maybe there is, and they just don't tell mortals about it," Brent joked.

"Could be. Stranger things have happened," she agreed.

Brent brought her up to speed on the attacks against hunters, the souped-up supernatural events, and their encounter with the vampire the night before.

"None of that sounds good," Cassidy agreed. "Sorren doesn't do daylight, so he's not here now. But if you give me the details, I can call him when he wakes up tonight and see what he's heard. Given how long he's been around, he's got a pretty impressive network of contacts. But I don't know how many of them are actually other vampires."

Brent knew that not all vampires or werewolves were automatically evil, and that many supernatural creatures remained wary of others for a variety of reasons.

"Have there been rumors about any organizations trying to recruit vampires? Especially groups with Church connections?" Brent asked.

"Gonna have to give me more to go on than that," Cassidy said. "Who do you suspect?"

Travis looked up as Brent laid out their suspicions that the attack could have been connected to the Sinistram and their theories on why. Although Travis had long-ago cut ties, Brent could see sadness and regret in the other man's face.

"Wow. That's quite a conspiracy theory," Cassidy replied. "Travis used to be with them, didn't he?"

"Yes, and the parting wasn't friendly," Brent answered. "But this isn't the kind of thing he could ask even if he was still a member in good standing. If there's some sort of alliance between the Sinistram and vampires, it's a big deal. Like, it goes against their sworn mission, and they're the Left Hand of the Holy Father."

"I know the Vatican has had its complicated politics over the centuries, but having the Pope collaborate with vampires would be a doozie," Cassidy said.

"That's putting it mildly," Brent responded. "We might be entirely off-base. It could totally be someone else. And it could be a splinter group within the Sinistram and not officially sanctioned. When we first considered it, we thought it was preposterous. Then we thought about it and realized it might not be as crazy as it seems."

"I'll ask Sorren," Cassidy promised. "And I'll check to see what any of our other contacts might have heard. Father Anne isn't Roman Catholic, but she knows a lot of clergy who are involved in the supernatural side of things."

"Last question," Brent said. "Have you heard more than usual about omens and augurs for the 'end of time'?"

Cassidy chuckled without humor. "There's always someone ready to lead the faithful up a mountain and wait for the apocalypse. Don't know why people still fall for it, but they do. I don't imagine that the recent black moon, lunar eclipse, and falling stars have helped. To people looking for signs, those all count. Even though they happen every year, and we're all still here."

"Travis says that the apocalypse is part of Sinistram lore. I'm just trying to rule out any connection."

"If I hear anything about that, I'll let you know."

"Thank you." Brent felt a little of the weight lift from his heart. Knowing they had powerful allies helped a lot. "Anything you find out will help."

He ended the call and looked at Travis. "It's a start. Get anywhere with your Night Vigil people?"

"I left messages or texts," Travis replied. "Like Sorren, a lot of them aren't daytime folks. The whole point of creating the network was to tap into what people with supernatural skills who weren't necessarily high-ranking or in charge of anything might know or hear. Your average shifter or witch on the street, so to speak."

Brent knew that at least a couple of the Night Vigil folks included young vampires and werewolves who were turned against their will and had sworn not to prey on humans. To survive, they banded together in loose-knit found families, where they were likely to hear gossip.

"I don't want to make them targets," Travis repeated. "I'm not asking anyone to go poking their noses into things. But what might seem like a random comment to them could end up meaning a lot more to us. It's worth a shot."

"I thought I'd see what Chiara Hamilton knows." Brent named another friend who was a source for supernatural intel. "She's usually plugged in."

"I'm going to check with some of the witches," Travis replied. "It's a long shot, but if there's a disturbance in the energies, they'll know."

Both men refilled their coffee and settled at the table. Brent called Chiara while Travis dialed the first of their witch friends.

"Hiya, Brent. To what world-ending situation can I attribute this?" Chiara greeted him. She lived north of Pittsburgh and usually worked with Mark Wojcik, but they had handled cases together and stayed in touch.

"Just wondering if you've heard of any supernatural conspiracies lately."

"Conspiracies?" she repeated. "You mean like Bigfoot working with UFOs?"

"Not exactly."

"What did you have in mind?"

"Groups teaming up that don't usually work together," Brent replied.

"Is this one of those things where if you give me more information, you'd have to kill me?" Chiara joked.

"Not exactly, but we don't want to put you in danger."

"That ship sailed a long time ago. I'm a big girl, and I know how to defend myself. Tell me what you need."

Brent gave her the basics, and she listened closely, remaining silent for a moment when he finished.

"There have been rumors of religious groups collaborating with vampires for a long time," she said finally. "I'm surprised Travis hasn't heard about them."

"I've heard of some," Travis chimed in. "But nothing recent or quite like what might be happening."

"Hmm," Chiara said, and Brent imagined her reaching for one of her research books. "Sometimes it was a local truce—don't eat our parishioners and we won't stake you. In other cases, there were mayors, governors, even a king or two who tried to recruit powerful vampires as bodyguards or partners in crime. It's usually offering protection in exchange for keeping other immortal threats at bay. Vampires don't need us to amass wealth, but they don't survive long when they try to wield direct power. The whole power-behind-the-throne angle has an appeal.

"As far as taking over a religious organization, there would be obstacles," Chiara speculated. "Not sure how they'd get around actually handling the sacred items like relics and holy water or holding mass. Those are deal-breakers for vamps."

She paused. "I've also heard that some of the 'doomsday prepper' folks have approached vampires about turning them if the apocalypse happens. I'm not sure why anyone would want to survive that, let alone become unable to die, but those folks don't usually make a lot of sense."

"Thank you," Brent agreed. "If you hear anything else, give me a call. And watch your back."

"Will do," she promised.

Brent ended the call and turned to Travis. "Do you think the upper echelon at the Sinistram would collaborate with vampires? And if they've been preparing for the world to end, would that change their game plan?"

"I took orders from them, but I was just one of their soldiers," Travis replied. "I wasn't privy to their secrets, and I didn't know the elders at all. Everyone in the organization was a priest, at least at one time. I guess it's possible that some were turned later and could avoid the sacred functions as part of management. It never occurred to me to wonder."

"Still a long shot," Brent cautioned. "And it doesn't explain how individual vampires could get away with not being caught. Could they handle holy stuff if they wore special gloves? They'd almost have to..." his voice drifted off as the enormity and horror of the possibility hit him.

"Take over the whole thing? Purge the regular humans and replace them with vampires?" Travis looked shell-shocked. "Yeah, I thought about that, too. Sounds crazy, but so do a lot of things that end up being true."

Travis and Brent took their dinner in Travis's apartment, and then Travis excused himself to make the rounds with Jon. He needed to check in with Matthew about clinic utilization, meet new residents, and spend a few minutes chatting with any of the halfway house folks who wanted his attention.

While Travis saw to the business of running the shelter, Brent made a fresh pot of coffee and settled in to scour what he thought of as the advance warning system. In reality, it was the tabloids dedicated to news of the weird, online sites for amateur monster trackers, and sensational chat boards for people who watched far too much *Scooby-Doo* as children.

Most of the discussion was utter dreck, with young men trying to top each other's made-up stories or attention-seekers giving their imaginations free rein. But now and then, tucked in among the ridiculousness, people actually had real run-ins with the supernatural.

He skimmed past the "Sasquatch ate my dog" reports, glossed over the vanishing hitchhiker stories, and ignored the UFO sightings.

Many of the stories repeated familiar tales, one write-up barely different from another. Brent suspected the posters had fun spinning their stories and reacting to the comments. Then one of the items caught his eye.

"That's different," he murmured. He chugged some coffee and

settled in to read. When Travis returned an hour later, Brent was ready. "I've found us a new case that might be related."

Travis looked curious and slightly amused. "Hit me with the details," He poured a cup of coffee and sat across from Brent.

"Ever hear of the town of Livermore?" Brent asked.

Travis shook his head. "Nope."

"How about the Conemaugh River Lake?"

"Maybe. Why?"

"Livermore was razed and flooded as part of the project to make the dam," Brent said. "There are a surprising number of old coal, timber, and railroad towns that got knocked down and covered with water when all the dams were built. Livermore just comes with more lore than most."

"Yeah?" Travis took a long gulp of hot coffee and savored the moment. Brent knew that while Travis tried hard to show his support and concern for St. Dismas's residents, the sheer volume of need often left him exhausted.

"The official record says that the town was badly damaged after several floods, which is part of why the dam was built there," Brent told him. "There were other factors as well—I'll spare you those details—but the dam seemed like the best alternative at the time. By the time they cleared the land, not many people were left to relocate. That's where the stories get interesting."

Brent warmed to the subject. "Some of them say that the town was flooded intact, but the buildings were actually torn down first. The cemetery, which isn't underwater, is said to be very haunted."

"That's interesting, but where's the case?" Travis asked. The back-and-forth was a familiar pattern, banter that both of them enjoyed.

"They say the lake is haunted by the ghost of a witch who lures people to their death," Brent replied. "Supposedly, she was a stubborn old lady who told fortunes and refused to leave when they cleared everyone else out, or she snuck back in afterward, the stories differ. Point being, she didn't leave when the waters rose and drowned. She cursed the builders of the dam and vowed that she would stay forever."

"Did she? Haunt the lake?" Travis took another gulp, and Brent could see how tired his friend was in the set of his shoulders.

"According to the urban legends, yes," Brent said. "There have been a series of unfortunate accidents since the lake was created. Boats capsized and the pilots drowned, that sort of thing. Probably happens at every lake, but the stories people told said that the ghostly form of a woman was seen nearby right before the tragedy, and that she could be heard wailing."

"Creepy. And probably mostly made up," Travis replied.

"Except that there have been three fatalities and two near-tragedies over the last couple of months," Brent pointed out. "And the last hunters who went to dispel her ended up dead. The official report says 'animal attack' but didn't specify what kind of animal, and the area isn't known for anything larger than deer. No bears, mountain lions, or wolves."

"And the cemetery?"

"People have claimed to see ghosts there since the dam was built. They also say they feel watched or just get a creepy feeling." Brent glanced at his notes. "No reported deaths or injuries. But there are other stories about a monster in the woods that sound more dangerous."

"Monster?" Travis finished his coffee, stood, and poured himself another cup.

"Ol' Red Eyes. He shows up to warn of looming catastrophe. Covered with dark fur, has bat wings, and red eyes," Brent said. "Sort of like the Mothman in West Virginia lore, but the stories don't say that he attacks anyone, just appears before something bad happens."

"Yet another omen," Travis said with a sigh.

"There's a lot of woods out there," Brent remarked, toying with his empty cup. "I know people go hunting and tramp around, but some of the territory is pretty rugged. It's not impossible that there are creatures who hide, especially if they have supernatural abilities."

"So do you want to go after the witch, or Ol' Red Eyes?" Travis asked.

Brent glanced at his partner to make sure he wasn't kidding, but Travis looked quite serious. "Let's deal with the witch, since her appearances are tied to recent fatal accidents and two dead hunters. We can check for Ol' Red Eyes afterward."

"What about the vampires?" Travis's fingers drummed on the lip of his mug.

"The dam is close enough we can go out and come back in daylight. Should keep the vamps off our tail while we wait to hear from Sorren and do a little more digging."

"Okay. Beats sitting around waiting for something to get the jump on us," Travis said. "Any reason we can't go tomorrow?"

Brent shook his head. "I've got a couple of new detective cases coming up, but not until next week. Gotta pay the rent. But tomorrow's open."

CHAPTER EIGHT

"IT'S SO PRETTY HERE," Brent remarked, taking in the green hills and blue water of the haunted lake.

The area offered a visitor's center, picnic area, hiking trails, sporting fields, pavilions for gatherings, and a history display. In the distance, Brent could see the Conemaugh Dam and hear the rush of falling water.

"Doesn't exactly look like a death trap," he commented as they walked toward the lake from where they parked.

"Good death traps rarely do," Travis said.

Signs warned boaters to be careful and made it clear that swimming was prohibited, but fishing was permitted. This early in the day, only a few kayakers and canoes dotted the lake's surface.

"It's a nice place," Brent said wistfully. "Maybe we can make it safer."

Someone had left a faded bouquet of flowers at the edge of the water, with a note commemorating the most recent boater to drown. Travis put his hands on his hips and surveyed the area. "It's way too big a lake for us to easily walk the whole way around it. Which is going to make it difficult to find any sign of the witch."

Brent scanned the shoreline. "Maybe not. Let's walk for a while and see if anything happens."

They had brought their usual protections: amulets, salt, and silver in their pockets, steel blades discreetly hidden beneath their jackets, and Travis's notebook of banishment spells and sigils. Brent had a shotgun with salt rounds and his Glock, while Travis carried his own handgun.

"Go ahead and listen for the ghosts," Brent told Travis. "I'll watch your back."

"I'll tell you what I hear," Travis replied. "I know it's a little weird having me report both sides of the conversation, but that way you know what they're telling me."

They found a spot in the shade, and Travis reached out to the ghosts, listening closely.

"The Livermore ghosts are faint, but there are a few that are stronger," Travis reported. "They might be the witch's most recent victims."

Brent drew his shotgun with salt rounds and kept watch while they stopped so Travis could focus on hearing what the ghosts could tell him.

"There's a man who looks like he was kayaking," Travis told Brent. "He says she flipped his kayak and dragged him under. Another ghost says the same thing happened to him."

"What about the others?"

Travis shook his head. "I think they're the hunters. Not dressed for boating, canvas jackets, flannel shirts, jeans, boots, they look like they knew how to handle trouble." He listened intently again.

"They're surprised I can hear them. They want me to stop the witch."

"We're hunters too," Travis told the hunters' ghosts. "Tell us what happened. Was it the witch?"

Travis listened again for a moment. "The taller one says they don't think the witch worked alone. They think another entity drew the witch here and made her stronger. Says they found binding sigils in the woods."

Travis returned his attention to the ghosts. "Did you use magic against her?"

"The tall ghost's companion replied, 'No. Salt and steel didn't work,'" Travis repeated so that Brent could follow the conversation.

Most hunters weren't able to talk to ghosts or do magic. They relied on shotguns, knives, salt, and a few rote incantations and rituals to banish low-level violent spirits and supernatural creatures. Usually, that was enough unless it wasn't.

"We have magic. Will you show us where the sigils are? And will you help us stop the witch?" Travis asked.

"We're ghosts. What can we do?" Travis repeated for Brent. "You'd be surprised," he replied to the ghosts.

Travis relayed the rest of the conversation to Brent, who had been keeping watch. "Did you see any other nasties out there?"

Brent shook his head. "No, although the lake and this whole area gives me the creeps. Maybe that's a warning."

"Let's go see the sigils, and I'll try to recruit more of the recent ghosts to give us a hand," Travis said.

"Having any luck?" Brent asked after they had walked for a while.

"The place is very haunted. Some are too faded to respond. Those probably include the people buried in the old Livermore cemetery," Travis replied. "We've got about half a dozen ghosts following us. They seem curious, but I don't know if they're willing to help."

"We want to stop the witch from killing people," Travis told the ghosts aloud, for Brent's sake.

Brent knew they couldn't do anything to prevent boating accidents brought about by carelessness or bad luck, but he figured maybe they could prevent the witch from adding to the death toll.

How? One of the ghosts spoke for the others, and Travis relayed the comment.

"We're going to break the sigils binding her here and do a ritual to send her away," Travis told them. "If she or anyone else tries to stop us, and you can interfere without getting hurt, we could use your help."

"Getting hurt? We're already dead," Travis repeated after one of the ghosts countered. Travis didn't try to correct him on all the ways it could still go wrong.

They headed for the sigil, which was carved into the bark of a large oak tree. Travis began to chant as Brent dug into the tree with his knife, cutting through the spelled drawing. Brent could feel the dark magic, but whether it was the power that bound the witch or the witch herself, he couldn't tell.

Travis raised his voice as the carving began to glow.

Brent felt the blade vibrate in his hand, growing hot. He held on, hissing against the pain, making the last few vital cuts. With the final swipe of the knife, the vibration stopped, and the sigil went dark. Brent blew out a breath and wiped the sweat from his forehead.

Travis looked to the hunters' ghosts. "Take us to the other sigils," he said aloud.

The hunters led them to two more trees with similar markings, positioned to triangulate on the lake, and Brent destroyed those sigils as well.

With the marks disabled, Travis turned his magic on the water witch.

A shriek of fury sounded, the shrill scream causing them to wince. A woman's figure rose from the center of the lake and hovered above the surface. She appeared to be made from water with long hair and a long dress. Fury twisted her expression, and rage glinted in her dark eyes. Brent leveled the shotgun, firing shells filled with salt and iron and blessed with holy water.

Her body exploded in a shower of water, but quickly reformed, looking even angrier.

Travis saw the ghosts hanging back. "We need your help," he

shouted to the spirits. "Help me fight her. Protect us. Stop the deaths."

The witch started toward Brent again, and he grabbed the propane torch that hung from a strap on his shoulder. He had modified its range so that he could send a stream of fire several feet through the air.

That drove the witch back, but Brent knew it couldn't hold her long, and Travis wasn't done yet with his incantation.

The spirits swarmed toward the witch, a wave of gray figures powered by anger. Travis kept chanting, and Brent dug a witch-banishing mark into the ground with his knife, then blasted it with fire.

The witch screamed again, hemmed in on all sides by the ghosts. The fire and sigil took a toll. She looked translucent, no longer solid, and her piercing scream no longer deafened everyone in range.

Two of the ghosts that made themselves visible to Brent surged toward the witch, one from each side. They plunged through the witch's water form, and when they met in the middle, both the ghosts and the witch vanished.

"Go in peace," Travis told the haunts, then he turned to his partner.

"Brent? You, okay?" Travis gently shook him by the shoulder.

"Yeah. Just...concentrating really hard," Brent replied. "I zoned out. I could actually *see* a couple of them."

"She's gone," Travis said. "No sign of the witch or her magic. If she was compelled to come here or stay against her will, I guess she went back to wherever she came from." Travis went still, listening for the ghosts. "A few of the ghosts stuck around, some moved on, and some just disappeared. I don't think they'll be bothering anyone."

Something drew Brent's attention to the edge of the forest. A dark form with red eyes stared out from the shadows before vanishing. "Do you see that?" He pointed.

"See what?" Travis looked in the same direction, but the manifestation was gone.

"I thought I saw something with red eyes under the trees," Brent replied.

"Certainly wouldn't be the first time we had multiple hauntings at the same place." Travis scanned the shadows warily. He laid down a fresh salt circle around the two of them, lit a candle, and pulled his flask of holy water from his pocket. "Be gone from here, all infernal and evil spirits. Depart from this place and do not return. Harm no one and take your eternal rest. Your presence is not wanted here. Go, and trouble this place no more."

A cold wind rose out of nowhere, sending a chill down Brent's back. Then mournful howls sounded from deep in the woods, feral as a wolf, a sound his hindbrain recognized as a mortal threat.

Three beasts burst from the tree cover, running at full speed. Despite their speed, Brent knew they weren't regular wolves, too large, too rangy, and with red eyes. They came at Brent and Travis with teeth bared and claws ready.

"Shit. I'm so done with this," Brent muttered.

Travis drew his Glock and fired a barrage of silver bullets that tore into the lead creature's chest, dropping it in its tracks and spraying black blood across the grass.

Brent still held the souped-up torch. He brandished the weapon, swinging the flame in an arc to keep the second and third monsters at a distance, but the tank was nearly empty, and it wouldn't last much longer.

The two creatures growled and bared their teeth, wary of the flames. Instead, they separated, circling in different directions, making sure Brent couldn't fend off both of them.

Travis shouted words of power that sent the two wolves flying backward. Before they could regain their footing, Travis blasted one with his shotgun, and Brent put a silver bullet right between the eyes of the third.

When the creatures fell to the ground and lay still, Travis and Brent approached warily, guns ready.

"Pretty sure they're dead." Brent took in the bullet-ridden bodies. "But what the hell were they?"

Travis walked around the corpses while still keeping his gun trained on them. "Not a normal wolf."

"Doesn't look like a werewolf," Brent mused. "At least, not the sort we've seen. The body and muzzle are all wrong."

"And they aren't shifting back to a human form," Travis noted. "Maybe cryptids of some sort got powered up by the spell that made the witch more dangerous."

"Might be the basis for the Ol' Red Eyes stories," Brent said.

"Maybe." Travis lifted his face to the wind, as if he were listening for the ghosts. "Do you know what they were?" he asked the spirits aloud.

"The ghosts think something drew them out of the deep woods," Travis told Brent a few moments later. "The only reason I can think of is to be a hunter trap, like powering up the witch. Trying to cause enough trouble to be sure hunters would come out to deal with it, and hope that it got them."

They thanked the ghosts and dragged the wolf-creatures to the edge of the tree line, hoping forest scavengers would deal with the bodies.

"I think we've overstayed our welcome," Travis replied. "Let's fall back before anything else charges out of the forest and figure out what the hell is going on."

They stayed on high alert, guns ready, and retreated to the car. Nothing tried to follow them, but Brent couldn't shake the feeling of being watched. Travis told him the ghosts had dissipated but remained nearby.

"That was a bit more than we bargained for," Travis said once they had put the lake behind them. "It's hard to know if the different hunts are connected." Travis drummed his fingers on the steering wheel. "There have been bursts of supernatural activity before that weren't part of a giant conspiracy. Sometimes it's the phase of the moon or the way the planets align, or fallout from some other para-normal incident."

"True," Brent replied. "But it's not just one situation, and even the ghosts thought there was another power involved. We're missing something big, something to pull it all together. I just can't figure out what."

Brent's phone rang. He looked down at the ID and frowned before answering on speakerphone, recognizing his unwelcome CHARON contact. "Shane?"

"Lawson. They're after me. I need—" An unnatural shriek sounded, drowning out the man's next words.

"—Todd Nature Reserve," Shane's voice came through, sounding scared and breathing hard, like he was running.

"Who's after you? What's going on?" Brent pressed. Travis pulled off the road and looked up the reserve on the GPS, indicating the distance and estimated drive time.

"You were right," Shane said. "Got set up—"

"Can you get to shelter? We're on our way." Brent glanced at the screen of Travis's phone as they got back on the highway, faster than the speed limit.

"Not gonna make it."

"Can you hide? Climb a tree?" Brent barely refrained from shouting into the phone. Travis gave him a worried look, then returned his attention to the road.

Shane's bloodcurdling scream made Brent wince.

"Shane! Shane!"

They heard another scream, a terrifying howl, and then what sounded like an animal licking its chops. Brent squeezed his eyes shut and tried not to throw up as he ended the call.

"Are you okay?" Travis asked after a few moments of silence.

Brent felt shaky and figured all the blood had drained from his face. He clutched the armrest white-knuckled as he tried to pull himself together.

"No. Can we—"

"Already adjusted the route," Travis assured him, giving the command to the GPS to head for Todd Nature Reserve. "But it's going to take at least half an hour to get there, not counting traffic."

"What do you think he meant when he said, 'you were right' and 'got set up'?" Travis was using the tone Brent always thought of as his confessional voice, quiet and calming.

"Shane hadn't believed me about a conspiracy to kill hunters," Brent replied. "I'm guessing that something changed his mind when it was too late to get away."

He took a few deep breaths. "Shane was an asshole, but I didn't want him dead. And if we're right, does this mean the Sinistram is going after CHARON as well as freelance hunters? That's like declaring war."

"I wish I knew," Travis replied. "Maybe when we hear from Sorren and the others, we'll be able to put the pieces together. As I recall, Sinistram and CHARON never liked each other or worked together voluntarily, but I always figured that was a power struggle or a turf war."

"I don't think CHARON liked any of the other groups," Brent said, feeling numb. "From their recruiting spiels, it always sounded as if they thought they were better hunters, trackers, better at handling ghosts and magic, the whole shebang. And from what you've said, Sinistram thought *they* were top of the heap. They were bound to clash."

"There's 'clashing' and then there's putting out a hit," Travis answered, his voice tight. "Until we figure this out, no one's safe."

Traffic had been slow, and by the time they reached the nature reserve, an ambulance and several police cars were already in the lot. Travis parked where they could easily get away, then he and Brent sauntered up like curious hikers.

"Sorry, the trails are closed until further notice," the cop blocking the entrance said. "We're still investigating, but it looks like a wild animal attack," the cop continued. "Don't want anyone else to get hurt."

Two men wheeled a stretcher out of the park and toward the ambulance. A blanket covered the body, including the face.

"What's happened?" Travis asked a nearby woman, looking believably innocent.

"I was jogging when I heard screams, and I called the police," she told him, wrapping her arms around herself for comfort. "I'm not surprised someone's dead."

"For everyone's safety, the park is closed while we investigate," the cop added. "I'd appreciate it if everyone could please clear out."

The woman made the sign of the cross and left for her car, and the others who had gathered drifted away.

"We're not going to get anything," Brent murmured. "The cops don't have a clue."

"They're not the only source of information," Travis said. "There are always ghosts. Maybe they saw something."

They went back to the car but didn't drive away. Brent watched as Travis closed his eyes and took a few deep breaths.

"Spirits of the nature reserve, if you saw what killed that man, please tell us what happened." He and Brent waited for a few minutes, long enough that he started to wonder if the ghosts would respond.

"We've got one," Travis said quietly. The ghost didn't make himself visible to Brent, but he could sense its presence.

"What killed that man? He was an...acquaintance...of ours," Travis asked.

They waited as the silence stretched on.

"It was one of the things that lives in the deep woods," Travis said finally, repeating what the ghost told him. "Even we rarely see them," he quoted. "But there was a power that urged it to attack."

"Urged?" Brent echoed. "Like magic?"

Another silence stretched, and Brent wondered if the ghost was trying to figure out how to explain.

"I don't know anything about magic," Travis repeated the ghost's words. "But the creature seemed...compelled. It hunted the man and killed him, then disappeared into the shadows. I have never seen that happen before."

"Were there other people nearby acting strangely?" Travis asked the ghost. "Someone who could have done something to attract the beast?"

"People come and go. I don't usually notice," Travis spoke the spirit's answer aloud then thanked the ghost and ended their connection. "Not sure that helped a lot."

Brent frowned, thinking. "We know that the attack wasn't natural and that whatever did it seemed to have been sent to kill Shane," he reframed what Travis had said. "But we don't know why Shane went to the nature reserve, and whether he found what he was looking for."

"Let's go back to St. Dismas. We can ask Shane himself."

Brent checked and re-checked the news on his phone as they drove. "There's a breaking news alert about a hiker's death and a possible dangerous wild animal, but no details. The park is closed until further notice pending an investigation and a search by Animal Control. They don't give Shane's name. Do you think whatever killed Shane will go after the Animal Control people?" Brent asked, looking up from his phone.

Travis thought for a moment before responding. "If the creature was sent to kill Shane, then probably not. The Animal Control people are already on alert for a dangerous wild animal. They aren't going to believe us if we try to warn them about a monster."

When they reached St. Dismas, Travis spoke quietly to Jon.

"I'll bring up a tray with dinner," Jon told them. "Glad you made it back safe and sound."

They thanked him and headed upstairs. "Figured it made sense for you to stay another night. Then we can check over your place to be sure it's safe," Travis said.

Brent hated to keep taking advantage of Travis's hospitality, but until they had a clearer idea of what they were up against, he agreed that there was safety in numbers. Once they got settled in Travis's apartment, they sat at the table while a fresh pot of coffee brewed.

"Can you reach him yet?" Brent asked.

Travis closed his eyes and concentrated. After a few moments, he seemed to find what he was searching for.

"Shane is still off-kilter, not surprising. Being dead takes some getting used to, and it can take a while for them to adjust," Travis replied. "What I can read right now is trauma, fear, shock, and betrayal. His words are still disjointed, but I get that he's certain it was intentional, and not a random attack."

Travis was silent for a few minutes. "Shane didn't recognize the creature, but it wasn't anything natural, so the whole bobcat or mountain lion thing doesn't fly."

Much as Brent disliked Shane, he would never wish his last moments to be filled with terror. "Is there anything we can do to ease his passage?"

"A prayer or two wouldn't hurt, but I'm not sure they'll help, either," Travis said. "I'll say a blessing and do a passing over ritual tonight. That might help settle his energy."

"If Shane felt betrayed and realized it wasn't a random attack, then it's likely it was connected to the other hunter deaths," Brent said. "And we need to figure out whether Sinistram is behind both of them."

"I don't think it's really a question of whether Sinistram is behind it; the question is, why?" Travis replied.

They stayed up a while after dinner playing cards, too jittery and unsettled to try going to sleep. Later, when Brent was alone in the guest room, he sensed Danny's spirit nearby.

"Are you safe?" Brent asked Danny, who shrugged.

"Be careful," Brent warned. "Someone is fucking around with ghosts. You can still get damaged, even though you're...dead." That last word stuck in his throat.

Danny placed a hand on his chest above his heart, a promise to be careful. Then he pointed to Brent and gave him a look that clearly demanded Brent also take precautions.

"I will. And if you can, watch my back, okay?" Brent replied.

He imagined that he heard the distant sound of Danny's laughter as the ghost blinked out.

CHAPTER NINE

"EVERYONE'S ON EDGE, but nobody's quite sure what's going on," Chiara Hamilton told Travis, somehow managing to sound upbeat despite the topic being catastrophic. "I've got contacts with a lot of different witches—brujas, *stregas*, and a Polish *vedmak*. Different traditions and talents. They're getting different pieces of the story, but I think it's all related."

Travis and Brent sat at the kitchen table in his apartment the next morning, each of them clutching hot cups of coffee like lifelines.

"Tell me what you hear." Travis had the phone on speaker between him and Brent.

"People have been having dreams, not just nightmares, more like prophetic sendings," she replied. "For some of my friends, that's not unknown, but it isn't common. They foresee great danger to the whole area around Pittsburgh, from dark magic as well as monsters."

"That's cheery," Brent murmured. Travis kicked him under the table.

"Can you narrow that down? Fire? Floods? Meteors from space?" Travis asked.

"Fire, which seems to be something from the past that is relevant again, although my contact wasn't sure how," Chiara said. "She saw people on fire and a silo blasted into the air. But she said it seemed like from a long time ago."

Brent took notes, letting Travis guide the conversation.

"What else?" Travis asked.

"People are paying attention to omens: stars, the moon, tea leaves, birds," she replied. "These aren't folks who normally watch those sorts of things. Now, they're taking them seriously, and they're worried."

Travis and Brent exchanged a look, and Travis knew they were both thinking about how often that topic had come up in the last couple of days.

"There's talk among the allied covens that someone is trying to stir up trouble between groups of practitioners, set them against each other," Chiara told him. "Still a shadowy 'they,' but it's been enough for the covens to issue warnings and do protective rituals. The interesting thing is it seems to be agitators who aren't from around here, instead of homegrown troublemakers."

Travis met Brent's eyes and knew they were thinking the same thing. *That could be Sinistram. It would fit.*

"I've heard that people from the city with minor supernatural abilities have been leaving the area, going to stay with friends, or just bugging out. There's a rumor that someone has put a bounty on people with paranormal skills. I hope it's not true, but folks are taking it seriously."

"They're right to be careful, and I wish I could give you a solid confirmation or denial," Travis replied. "We think a group is going after cryptids and witches. Not sure about other talents, but better safe than sorry."

"The witches and people with abilities who are staying are banding together," Chiara said. "Even some of the werewolves and vampires who are on the straight-and-narrow have joined us. They said they'd rather work with the hunters than take their chances on whoever is behind the crackdown."

If he and Brent were correct about Sinistram's role, those instincts were spot on.

"That's all I've got for now, but I'll keep my ears open," Chiara said. "We're kinda running an unofficial supernatural sanctuary until things cool down."

"Thank you," Travis said. "For the info and for helping protect the community."

"No problem," she said with forced humor. "We weirdos have to stick together."

After the call ended, Travis found himself lost in thought, staring at the wall until Brent cleared his throat.

"That was interesting," Brent remarked. "The witches and the monsters are scared. And we still don't have a plan to fix things."

Travis checked for missed calls. "Nothing yet from Cassidy. Let's try a long shot and see if any of the recently dead Sinistram priests know anything they want to share."

Brent raised an eyebrow. "Do you think they'd tell you?"

Travis shrugged. "They're beyond retribution from the elders. Maybe there's something they want to get off their chests. I can still hear Confession."

As Travis meditated to prepare, Brent went through the familiar checklist of assembling what he would need to recover afterward: water, orange juice, a muffin, and peanut butter crackers to provide sugar, protein, and hydration.

After several minutes, Travis opened his eyes, and Brent sat across from him again, taking both of his hands. Just in case the spirits were not friendly, Brent had salt and iron handy to break Travis's connection.

"Ready?" Travis felt certain that Brent could see the hesitation in his face. He didn't mind doing a séance, but he had little desire for contact with Sinistram members, living or dead.

"No, but what the hell."

"They'll talk to me, and I'll relay what I hear, but you won't hear the actual ghosts," he reminded Brent.

"Which is creepy as fuck, but I get it," Brent replied.

He had referred to the spirits speaking through Travis as being a sock puppet on more than one occasion, and Travis had to admit that his partner wasn't completely wrong.

"Priests of the Sinistram, hear me," Travis said in deep, measured tones. His eyes were shut, leaving it to Brent to keep watch for any real-world threats. "I wish to speak with you."

They sat for a moment in silence, and then he spoke again. "Brothers of the collar, I seek your wisdom," Travis said. "I need to know who has corrupted the Order."

He was taking a chance making that leap, but he gambled on two things. First, that the ghosts no longer feared retribution, and second, that those who had been with the group long enough to die of old age might deeply resent major changes that ran counter to their mission.

I knew you, Travis Dominick. You left us. Why do you seek us out now? Travis heard the voice in his mind and repeated the comment for Brent's sake.

Travis recognized the man, whom he knew as Brother Benjamin, one of the senior priests who presided at his acceptance into the Sinistram back in the day.

"Because I believe something fundamental has changed, and people are dying," Travis replied out loud, unwilling to get bogged down over old differences. "Is it true that vampires have infiltrated the brotherhood?" Travis sat in silence for several minutes, waiting for the ghost to answer. He wondered if the ghost would feel guilt over betraying a secret, even if he opposed the change, or whether he might see this as a way to right a wrong.

Yes. It is true.

Two other ghosts had joined them, elderly priests Travis vaguely remembered from his time with the group, Brother Andrew and Brother Frank. They would have been ranked high enough to be in the governing body and privy to its secrets. He described what he saw to Brent.

"What happened, and why was that permitted?" Travis tried to word his questions neutrally, avoiding blame to keep from pissing off his ghostly informants.

Those at the very top wanted more power, Brother Andrew replied. *They sought out the vampires, and many of them permitted themselves to be turned. I refused, spoke out against the change, and died.*

Brother Frank's ghost nodded. *They sought power beyond death. And they wanted to finally be rid of the hunters who interfered with the supremacy of the supernatural.*

The phrase "supremacy of the supernatural" sent a chill down Travis's spine. "They wanted to dominate those without abilities?" he clarified aloud.

Yes. They felt it was their due since they were powerful with magic, and then deathless after being turned, Brother Benjamin replied. *They resented that independent hunters defied reporting to the Sinistram and doing their bidding, and they were angry that "mere" mortals dared to kill creatures and rein in supernatural abilities.*

Travis had braced himself for exactly that kind of admission, but hearing it confirmed made him simultaneously furious and heartbroken at the treachery. He remembered the fragmentary images he had picked up from Shane's ghost and suspected he now knew why the CHARON agent had felt betrayed. Brent looked shocked and angry when Travis relayed the ghosts' words.

"Did the Sinistram put a bounty on hunters? And did that include killing members of CHARON?" Travis asked.

Travis had been speaking his questions and the ghosts' answers aloud for Brent's benefit, and on this last inquiry, he felt Brent's hands tighten on his.

Yes. It was discussed before my death and implemented afterward.

Travis felt sick to his stomach. "Everywhere, or just the Pittsburgh Chapter? Does it go all the way to the Vatican?" Several tense moments passed before the answer came.

No. Other chapters were not involved yet. Neither was the Holy

Father, although there might have been some traitors in Rome who knew and did nothing, Brother Andrew said.

One problem at a time. And Pittsburgh's chapter is a big enough battle without taking on the Vatican, Travis thought.

"How do we stop them?" he asked.

Saving our chapter is beyond hope, I fear, Brother Frank said. *But if you can expose them, it may stop the rot from spreading to other cities.*

More importantly, stop their plans, Brother Benjamin interposed. *They want the monsters to be dominant. That will leave humans without magic or supernatural abilities to be...food. They are waking the old ones. If they succeed, stopping them may no longer be possible.*

"Old ones?" Travis asked. "Who are the old ones?"

Creatures who have slumbered for centuries, or remained hidden in the depths of the forest, the ground, and the water, Brother Andrew replied. *They were content to stay in the shadows, but they will not turn down the chance to become ascendant once more, as they were before humans came to the fore.*

Travis was tiring, and he could feel that the ghosts were slipping from his grasp. "Thank you. We will do everything we can to stop the monsters and keep people from dying."

We wish you luck, although we cannot see the outcome, Brother Benjamin replied.

With that, Travis let go of his connection to the ghosts and slumped forward onto his elbows.

Brent pressed a bottle of orange juice into his hand. "Drink. I've got something for you to eat after that. When you're ready, I'll help you to the couch."

Travis accepted the juice gratefully and downed it, then tried to eat the muffin slowly so it didn't come back up. "Did you hear all that?"

"Not everything, but enough," Brent said in a grim tone. "Sometimes it sucks to be right."

Travis managed to make it to the couch without having to lean too hard on Brent. "Well, that explains why the whole section on vampires and necromancers was missing from the Sinistram library the last time I visited." Travis felt the grueling aftereffects of the ghostly conversation. "They might have been afraid someone would find something in the books that could work against them."

"I'm going to make another pot of coffee and settle in to do some research while you sleep that off," Brent told him. "Give me your phone. I'll wake you if Cassidy returns your call, but everyone else can wait. Rest, and then we can debrief."

Travis wanted to argue, but he ended up mumbling something incoherent as he sat on the couch and fell to one side.

"Rest." Brent pulled Travis's legs up on the cushion and spread a throw over him. "I'm not going anywhere, and I won't let anything get to you."

Travis wanted to point out that Brent couldn't protect him from ghosts or visions, but he fell asleep before he could.

———

"WHAT TIME IS IT?" Travis came around slowly, unsure whether he was actually waking or in a very realistic vision.

"A better question is, what day?" Brent handed him a hot cup of coffee. "You slept all night and half of the next morning. From what you were muttering, I gather it wasn't all peaceful. Did you have visions? Share with the class when you wake up. I found some interesting stuff, too. And before you ask, Cassidy said Sorren should return tonight, and he had information for us."

"That...can't be good." Travis sipped his coffee and tried to reorient himself.

"Maybe we already know the worst about Sinistram," Brent said. "I'm hoping Cassidy and Sorren can clue us in to how the vampire faction managed that. It's rather discouraging to know that politics doesn't end even after you're dead."

"True." Travis willed the hot liquid to send his blood rushing and clear the fuzz from his mind. "I'll tell you about the visions I had while I was sleeping, but I need to make sense of them myself first. How about you catch me up on what you've been doing while I've been out."

"I need more coffee for that." Brent got up and refilled their cups, then returned to his seat.

"The early warning system is going absolutely bonkers with stories," Brent said, meaning the tabloids, podcasts, and social media sites dedicated to supernatural conspiracies. "Plenty of sightings of Ol' Red Eyes. Either there are dozens of him, or he can teleport, because they're claiming he's popping up all over."

"More omens," Travis said.

"No kidding. Everyone and their brother is seeing signs in frogs, owls, spiders, pretty much everything. Then there's the big story about a sea monster in the Monongahela River."

"Seriously?" Travis lifted his head and looked at Brent to make sure he wasn't joking.

"I couldn't dream this stuff up if I tried." Brent crossed his heart. "People say they have seen a huge serpent in the river and that it's damaged boats and caused problems for river traffic. Of course, that immediately spawned websites selling amulets and preachers rushing to the waterfront to pray it away."

"Some things never change," Travis agreed.

"Not sure yet whether or not there's any truth, but even the regular media is running segments on it. If Loch Ness has Nessie, would this be 'Messie' in the Mon?" Brent asked with a grin.

"Ugh. There's got to be a better name."

"You'd think so," Brent agreed. "Photos are showing up online that claim to be of the river creature. That stuff is easy to fake—especially with AI—but I'm hearing back-channel chatter from hunters that makes me think there's some truth to the rumor."

Travis stood behind Brent as he called up news sites reporting on the sea serpent. A couple of vendors wandered along the riverbank selling charms to the crowd that gathered along the riverside while a minister led a prayer group nearby.

"Nearly capsized my boat," a man told the reporter. "Like in one of those movies. Couldn't see all of it, but it was big around and long."

"There's a temporary halt on small, non-commercial craft on the river until authorities get to the root of the problem," the reporter said, looking into the camera with the river behind him.

"Larger boats are heavily cautioned. We're told that authorities have brought in sonar and other technology to see into the deepest water. The city has promised to keep river traffic running, but we'll have to wait and see whether they can deliver on that promise."

Brent clicked away, and Travis sat. "How is that even possible with all the locks and dams on the river?" Travis asked.

Brent shrugged. "If something magicked the creature into the river, that wouldn't matter. It's certainly not native. And if it's supernatural, it might have other ways to get around obstacles."

"Maybe that's what the priests meant by old ones," Travis mused. "And if they really are waking up, how do we put them back to sleep?"

"If the Sinistram witch vampires are working dark magic to rile up the creatures and attack hunters, stopping the magic might make the monsters go back to sleep," Brent suggested.

"Maybe. I hope so, because I don't know how to fight a sea serpent."

"I've also got a lead on that vision you had about the fires and the canister being blasted into the air." Brent turned his laptop so Travis could see old black-and-white newspaper photos showing a blasted stretch of a city street.

"What is this?" Travis asked.

"The Equitable Gas Explosion of 1927," Brent replied. "A big natural gas storage facility blew up and took a chunk of houses with it. Best anyone can figure, the company thought the tanks were completely empty before workmen tried to weld leaks shut, but there was enough gas still left to blow everything sky high. People died, city blocks had to be razed, and it broke windows a mile away."

"Let me guess, it also sent one of those tanks up like a rocket."

"Yep," Brent confirmed. "But the area hasn't been a hotbed of haunting, at least from anything I could find. So why did you see that particular disaster?"

Travis studied his coffee as if it held the secrets of the universe. "We've looked into several mine disasters, which could also fit the 'old ones' when there have also been monsters. Some of those involved fires. Now the natural gas disaster. Maybe the pattern isn't just the ghosts, it's the harrowing by fire."

"That doesn't sound good."

Travis knocked back the rest of his drink. "Fire cleanses. It's not just Biblical, it's part of a lot of ancient lore. Suppose you're a group of ancient vampire priests who want to scour minor monsters and enough pesky mortals from the area so no one challenges your power. First, you summon the old ones, terrify everyone, then wipe them away with cleansing fire, and you're the hero to the passive saps that are left."

"That's crazy enough, it might just be a theory." Brent looked vaguely ill at the prospect. He quickly typed into a search engine, and his eyes widened at the response.

"Most of the state's natural gas production happens in Western PA, near Pittsburgh. Plenty of wells, capped and active, and storage facilities housed in underground formations like salt caverns," Brent read aloud.

"Great."

"It gets worse," Brent said, "since the oil and gas industry has been in this area for so long, there are a lot of orphaned and abandoned oil and gas wells. Most of them haven't been capped. For others, the location is no longer known."

"How many are we talking about?" Travis felt a chill go down his spine.

"Official estimates say 300,000 to 700,000 orphaned and abandoned wells, but no one really knows for sure." Brent sounded stunned. "Not counting all those coal mines, and no one even has a complete map of where they are."

"Fuck. That's like living on top of a time bomb."

"Yeah. The wells and mines leak methane and other bad chemicals, catch fire, and can explode. And they're fuckin' *everywhere*," Brent said.

"Any other good news, while I was sleeping?"

Brent looked like he wished he could spike his coffee. At the moment, Travis was also regretting his no-alcohol policy.

"Just that there are at least twelve decommissioned Nike missile sites in and around Pittsburgh. The missiles were supposed to be removed, but..."

"Missiles?" Travis echoed, appalled. "Were they—"

"Some carried explosive payloads. Others had nukes."

"Oh my God."

"And there's an active nuclear power plant twenty-seven miles from Pittsburgh," Brent said. "I mean, we got through the Cold War and the Russians didn't blow us up, so maybe it's not worth worrying about."

"But they weren't crazy-religious vampire ninja priests," Travis replied, a weak attempt at humor in the face of potential annihilation. "You'd think stuff like this would lower property values."

"Far as I can tell, most people have no idea about the mines, the wells, or the missile sites, and the power plant keeps a low profile."

Travis rose and started to pace. "Shit, shit, shit." He stopped and looked at Brent, wishing he would wake up and discover this was all a bad dream. "What the hell do we do? This is so far above our pay grade—"

"If we can stop Sinistram, we don't have to deal with the explosives." Brent sounded calm, but Travis could see the twitch in his partner's jaw that revealed how hard he was clenching his teeth.

"Guess that's what we're gonna have to do then."

"Did you get dreams or visions while you were sleeping?" Brent asked. "We're grasping at straws here, so every little bit of information counts."

"I dreamed about a large open field with the night sky overhead," Travis replied. "It looked like stars were falling, don't know whether that was meteors or space junk. It should have been pretty, but it made me shiver."

"More omens," Brent said.

Travis nodded. "Then tongues of fire burst out from the lawn, shooting up into the air. That's when I woke up."

Brent took another swig of his coffee. "Yeah, nothing creepy about that at all," he said sarcastically.

"And I saw a book," Travis went on. "It's been in some of the other visions, very old, looks like a book of spells. But not one that I've seen at the Sinistram library. I'm not sure what to make of that."

Travis's phone rang, making him jump. When he realized the call came from Cassidy, he glanced at the window, unaware that the sun was already down.

"Hi, Travis, Brent. I have Sorren here with me," Cassidy told them. "I'll put him on speaker."

"Travis, Cassidy said you had questions?" Sorren's voice was deep and soothing, and Travis wondered whether it had sounded like that in life or if that was a vampire adaptation.

"Thanks for calling me back. Have you heard anything about vampires infiltrating and taking over the Pittsburgh chapter of Sinistram?" No matter how often he said it out loud, it still sounded absurd.

Sorren didn't answer right away. Travis and Brent exchanged a look, and Travis wondered if he had exceeded the vampire's patience and made him think this was a prank.

"It's possible," Sorren replied a moment later. "My kind are more solitary now than we were in life, and we tend to avoid groupings, because they present a target. But there are radical factions, something that, unfortunately, didn't end with being mortal." Another pause. "Tell me what you've learned, or suspect. If I know anything, I will confirm."

Travis and Brent took turns laying out what they had discovered, as well as their theory on what the vampire-infiltrated Sinistram stood to gain.

"I know that sounds crazy—" Brent said.

"Less so than you might think." Sorren sounded worried, which made Travis even more apprehensive. "While I considered such plans to be improbable, what you've pieced together is in line with rumors I've heard about the more fanatical players."

Sorren paused. "Vampires are just people with special abilities. Unfortunately, the 'dark gift' doesn't convey special wisdom along with the speed and strength. Vampires can be just as susceptible to misinformation and conspiracy theories as mortals.

"What you're talking about sounds very much like a theory that I've heard mentioned over the years. I've never paid much attention to it myself, but apparently others did," Sorren went on. "There was a monk in the 1700s who was said by some to be a prophet, and was widely also believed to be a vampire. His rantings were ignored by the Vatican, but they may have found their way to the Sinistram."

"What did he believe?" Travis asked.

"He believed that the literal end of the world was coming, and that the only survivors would be vampires. After the end of everything on earth, the vampires would ascend to become demigods. I'm not sure what good that does if everyone else is dead, but that didn't seem to deter believers," Sorren said. "There were rumors of apostate vampire priests who looked forward to the Apocalypse and saw it as the eventual triumph of immortals over mortals."

Sorren's expression of distaste made his opinion clear. "I've outlived enough prophets to see their prophecies proven wrong. But there's always a group that buys into that kind of thing enough that they sell all their possessions and go sit on top of a mountain waiting to be taken away from the stress of mortal life—only to end up deeply disappointed."

"The elders chose to be turned into vampires so they would 'survive' the end of the world?" Brent echoed. "That's dingo-ate-my-baby crazy."

"Wouldn't be the first time a crazy idea caught hold," Sorren observed.

"I can see how the Sinistram elders could have found that appealing," Travis said after a moment to think about what Sorren had said. "After all, they loved feeling more special than regular people and knowing secrets. And it's definitely got roots in the idea that 'believers' would survive the ultimate destruction and take over a purified world."

"The crazy just keeps on coming," Brent muttered.

"How do we stop them?" Travis asked.

"With a team," Sorren replied. "I will gather some allies here. I'd suggest putting together your most trusted witches and people with supernatural abilities. If we each take on the Sinistram from our respective strengths, we stand a good chance of overturning their control."

"I have a couple of powerful witches who will help, and Archibald Donnelly, who's a necromancer," Sorren went on. "I know you have a number of people who have fought beside you against prior threats. We don't need an army. We just need to hit the right weak points hard."

"Okay," Travis said. "How do we figure out the plan and the timing?"

"We'll call you back at midnight," Sorren said. "Let's see what's come together by then."

Travis stared at his phone after Sorren ended the call, then looked at Brent, feeling adrift. "I guess a slim chance is better than no chance at all, right?" He gave a weak smile.

"We can't just call people and ask them to stand by for the end of the world," Brent said. "Who do we know who has gifts and might be able to help in a fight?"

Travis made a list of the people from his Night Vigil with precognition, visions, omens, as well as magic. The team he had assembled wanted to use their abilities for good, and Travis paid them a small stipend for being part of the team. The ghostly part of the Night Vigil surrounded the St. Dismas church and halfway house, frightening away ruffians.

"Angie and Roger are in," Travis reported. Angie got glimpses of the future, and Roger saw omens. Both had called him, having gotten an insight that something big was brewing and offering to help, a testimony to their abilities.

"Aricella says she'll rally the covens," Brent set down his phone to take a sip of coffee.

"Good. I know Sorren said he'd bring Archibald Donnelly with him, but I was going to give Dr. Peters a call anyhow. Two necromancers are better than one, and although vampires don't like to admit it, they are technically still dead," Travis replied.

"How about I call Peters, and you call Father Jacinski and Father Leo, see if we can get any backing from the Occulatum or the Logonje?" Brent said.

If the Sinistram was the Church's black ops, the Occulatum was its FBI, less extreme and more attuned to stopping supernatural threats. Priests from the Occulatum often helped out local monster hunters. The Logonje were Polish priests with arcane abilities, and Jacinski was part of that group as well. He was located in Pittsburgh, although Travis and Brent hadn't worked with him in a while.

After a couple of hours, Brent set his phone aside and let out a deep breath. "Well, that's everyone on my list. They're on standby and said they'd been expecting a call since the sea monster showed up."

"A benefit to knowing so many people with pre-cog," Travis observed. "Jacinski and Leo said they'll check with other priests they trust in the Occulatum and Logonje to see what people have heard and who can help."

They still had several hours before Sorren was due to check in, so Brent went back to monitoring the news while Travis opened up the

Dark Web, a corner of the Internet specializing in questionable supernatural information. Ensorcelled encryption was supposed to protect users from picking up a demonic virus or dark magic file corruption. The people and information were notoriously dodgy, and Travis only risked the danger when the situation was dire.

"Hey, I think I might have something," Travis said after a while. "I'm on the Dark Web—don't judge. Desperate times, desperate measures."

"As long as you exorcise your own computer if it gets possessed," Brent replied.

"Yeah, yeah. But I remembered that some of the priests I knew in the Sinistram went online even though they weren't supposed to, including me," he confessed. "As far as I know, the others stayed with the Order. So...I thought I'd see what they're talking about."

"And?" Brent sounded intrigued.

"I found them in an 'End of Days' conversation thread. But get this, one of them let slip that his organization had been preparing for an apocalypse that hasn't come, and so they've started to question whether a cleansing or reboot is needed and if they should start it," Travis told him.

"He said they feel like they wasted their preparations, but then they realized that instead of stopping an apocalypse to protect humanity, they could cause one to cull the number of humans and make them subservient to the higher-level immortals," Travis reported. "He was also pretty clear that they also have a distaste for the lesser monsters but see them as useful for culling the humans."

"He just put that out there? Said the quiet part out loud?" Brent said, incredulous.

"Guess he figured he was among friends," Travis replied. "But think about that, it's the missing piece to explain the 'why.' They got tired of being on standby, so they decided to bring the End of Days about themselves and use it for their own ends."

"Regardless of how many people it killed."

"The Sinistram never let the little details get in their way," Travis answered, with an expression that made his disgust clear.

"Wow. That's...psycho."

"The Sinistram keeps being even worse than my lowest expectations," Travis said.

Brent slid his cold coffee to the side. "While you were figuring out the 'why,' I think I got the 'where.' Ever heard of Moraine State Park?"

Travis shook his head. "Should I have?"

"It's a bit north of the city. Nowadays, it's got a lake and is popular for picnics and boating. But it's built on reclaimed land that has 422 capped oil and gas wells and 53 coal shaft mines. Oh, and there's an abandoned missile silo at one end too," Brent said.

"That's a lot of potential firepower all in one place."

Brent nodded. "That's what I was thinking. And it's haunted. Abandoned cemeteries, a creature with red eyes, a woman in white, and soldier ghosts. Plus green orbs and white flashes. Spooky."

"Setting off the wells there might not kickstart the entire Apocalypse, but it would definitely be a good start," Travis said.

Brent skimmed the page he was reading and quickly jumped to a couple of other sites. "Wow. I guess the surprising part is that there hasn't been an apocalypse there yet." He let out a low whistle. "Apparently, the area that is now the park has had a shadow over it for a long time. This article says that the first tribes talked about a place where the 'ice fingers,' glaciers, left barrows filled with ancient monsters."

"Barrows?"

"When glaciers push up a bunch of loose rock and leave it behind when they melt, those piles are called 'moraines,' hence the park name," Brent said. "According to the lore, people have said for a long time that there's powerful, primordial magic deep in the land that has a darkness to it. I guess people with abilities have avoided the area for a long time. And a couple of legends said that the power of the land's magic made it a locus for a final reckoning," he read from the screen.

"Yeah, but that didn't stop the railroads, the oil or gas companies, or the coal mines," Travis countered.

Brent shrugged. "Think about it. In a way, all of those very dangerous types of work might have actually been *attracted* there if the land wanted blood. Those jobs all have a lot of fatal accidents."

"Yeah, I can see that," Travis agreed. "Plus, the jobs didn't pay well, so that would lead to other problems."

Brent nodded. "The small towns that are under the lake now had a reputation for fights, drinking too much, and suicides. Anyone who could leave, did."

"What else?" Travis asked, intrigued. "I've lived here my whole life and never heard any of that, although people have mentioned the park for things like company picnics and weddings."

"Nowadays, that's how people think of the area," Brent confirmed. "Did you know that back in the first half of the 1900s, there was even an amusement park on the land that's now under the lake? It had rides, a dance hall, skating rink, bandstand, and picnic pavilions."

"Let me guess, things didn't go well?"

"There were accidents and deaths." Brent skimmed the text. "People started to say it was unlucky or cursed. When it shut down, arson burned most of the buildings, but the metal rides were out there in the woods for a long time."

"There's nothing creepier than an abandoned amusement park." Travis shivered.

"I've got to agree with you," Brent replied.

"All that's gone now, right?" Travis asked.

"When the wells and mines petered out, the railroad stopped running, and there weren't any jobs, so people left." Brent chuckled. "Interesting phrasing, people called the rich men who owned the mines, wells, and railroads, 'vampires' because they sucked the life out of the communities."

"They weren't wrong."

"Then in the 1950s, the land was bought to create a park and build a lake. What was left of seven towns was razed and flooded, including all but a few cemeteries." Brent sounded excited about his findings. "Locals still said the area was haunted. People drowned in the new lake, and campers said there were ghosts and vampires in the forest."

"Sounds a lot like what we went up against at Livermore," Brent added. "Is there a haunted town under every man-made lake? It sure seems like it."

While Brent talked, Travis did some searches of his own. "Huh. The chat boards for apocalypse watchers have glommed onto Moraine. They're chock-full of stories of omens, sightings, and predictions from psychics."

He fell silent as he read for a moment. "According to the chatter, between the natural dark magic and all the death and destruction, it's fed the area's power, with the park and the lake as the nexus. One person wrote, 'all that was buried will be revealed.'"

"That's not worrisome at all," Brent replied.

"It's a good reason for the park to be the 'where' for the disaster," Travis said. "There's inherent dark power, a history of tragedy, angry ghosts, and maybe some ties to vampires."

"And releasing all the stored power of those capped wells and mines, and the twisted magic, would certainly feel like the End of Days to anyone nearby," Brent agreed. "Might even be enough to trigger other explosions, set off some sort of chain reaction."

A knock at the door broke off their conversation. Jon stuck his head inside.

"Travis, there's a man standing outside beyond the wards like he can't cross them. He's dressed like a monk and says he wants to speak with you."

Brent turned to Travis. "A monk?"

One of the Keepers from the library? No way, Travis thought, but as soon as the words crossed his mind, he knew it was true, however unlikely.

"I'll be right there," Travis told Jon, who nodded and withdrew.

Brent put a hand on Travis's arm as he moved to rise. "It could be a trap."

"Don't worry. I'm not going to invite him in or go past the wards. But if my hunch is right, this might be the missing piece we need."

At this point in the evening, the community rooms were dark and empty. Curfew was near, and most residents welcomed the quiet.

Jon waited for him by the door, armed with a silver crucifix, a wooden stake, and a high-powered rifle. Brent stood next to him, equally well-armed, where he could step in if needed.

"Glad you're prepared," Travis said, and Jon gave him a nod.

"Gotta be ready for everything," Jon replied.

Travis opened the door and walked out onto the top step. The man on the other side of the sidewalk wore a brown, hooded robe with a knotted rope belt. Travis recognized the outfit immediately from the Sinistram library, and when the man raised his head, he knew he had seen the Keeper before, on his most recent visit.

"Father Dominick," the Keeper greeted him. "Dire times are upon us. Choices have been made that many oppose. The elders have been replaced with immortals, vampires, ancient witches, shifters, and others. I have brought you something that may help. You will need it to stop the End of Days."

From beneath the voluminous sleeves of his robe, the man produced a leather-bound book that looked exactly like the one from Travis's dreams.

"From the missing section you inquired about," the Keeper replied with the barest hint of bitter humor in his voice.

"Thank you, but I have to ask, why now? And if others oppose the...regime change...why haven't you gone against the elders?" Travis remained alert for treachery, but neither the protective ghosts nor his own intuition suggested the situation was other than what it seemed.

"Their protections are too strong," the Keeper replied. "And our vows carry a compulsion. I bring you this at the risk of my life for breaking my vows. I'm trusting you to do what we cannot."

At that, the Keeper placed the book on the ground, turned away, and vanished into the darkness.

Travis waited for a moment, alert for trickery, but when the ghosts assured him that no one was lurking to attack, he hurried down the steps to take the book. He felt a frisson of magic as soon as he touched the tome, and quickly returned to the sanctuary behind the protective wards.

Jon had stepped outside to cover him and had brought out a steel-sided, warded case that they used for hazardous relics. Travis put the book inside and felt the buzz of power end.

They moved back inside to where Brent waited in the lobby, gun in hand.

"Who was that?" Jon looked up and down the street to make sure they weren't about to be besieged.

"A Keeper, one of the librarians at the Sinistram library," Travis told him. "They're pretty creepy, and they've usually made it clear that while they will assist me, they disapprove that I left the Order. That guy helped me the last time I was there, when I noticed all the vampire books were missing."

"What did he bring you?" Brent eyed the box warily.

"I haven't had a chance to look, but I felt the magic when I picked it up," Travis said.

"Do we need to contain it?" Jon looked askance at the case as if the book inside might attack.

"He said it put him at great risk to break his vows and bring me the book," Travis said. "But even if it's not a trap, magic is dangerous. Let me get a space prepared so I can study it in a 'bubble.'"

Jon waited with the case while Travis and Brent went back upstairs and cleared everything from the kitchen table. Travis said protective spells while Brent set down a salt circle and marked sigils to banish evil. Jon brought the box to the door and watched from a safe distance.

"Everything okay?" Jon asked.

Travis nodded. "Yeah. I think the real danger is what's *in* the book, not the book itself. There's something that the new bosses at the Sinistram didn't want anyone to know, and I can't wait to find out what it is."

He checked his watch. They still had two hours until they were due to talk with Cassidy and Sorren. "With luck, I might stumble on something useful by the time we do our call."

"Let me know if you need anything," Jon said. "I'll close up for the night."

Brent checked the coffee pot and made fresh. "How can I help?"

"Have my back," Travis said. "If something goes haywire, call Aricella. With the wards, whatever happens should be contained inside the space, but if I get hurt, I might not be able to shut it down."

"I've got you," Brent promised.

Brent took a seat outside the warded space and cradled a fresh cup of coffee in his hands as he watched Travis don spelled gloves and remove the book from the protective container.

"It's old," Travis narrated. "Leather binding, I don't want to know what kind of skin."

"Ew."

Travis shrugged. "We've both heard the stories." While many people dismissed the legends as being spread by those against any kind of supernatural power, the rumors remained that dark grimoires were often wrapped in covers made of human skin.

He carefully opened the thick book, murmuring a protection spell as he did so. Nothing happened, but he looked at the yellowed pages and fine script and hoped that the ink wasn't mixed with blood.

"Anything?" Brent asked.

"Good penmanship," Travis quipped. "The book is really old. I'm going to need to go slow so I don't damage anything."

"Can you pick up anything with your other senses?"

"I've clamped down on getting any sort of reading on the energy until I know what we're dealing with," Travis said.

"Good idea."

Despite his precautions, Travis could feel the tingle of magic as he handled the book, even through the spelled gloves. Some of the text was in Latin and some in English, but the archaic script made for slow reading, and Travis needed to make sure he fully understood the text.

"The volume is called the Precepts," he said after a long silence. "It's a study of how the magic of vampirism works. The author holds that the fundamental magic underlying vampires, werewolves, and shifters is very old, going back to the formation of the world and possibly the universe."

"Okay, interesting but not a revelation," Brent said.

"The book is essentially forensic magic," Travis added. "The author wanted to know why vampires could live on blood and no other nourishment. It's quite a long treatise. That's the foundation. From there, he looks at how the ancient magic creates immortality and the other vampire traits like super speed and strength."

"I'm sure it's fascinating, but why did Sinistram's high command think they needed to hide it?"

"I haven't gotten through everything, but from what I see, there are spells and rituals to break a vampire's magic," Travis replied.

"Turn them back to mortal?" Brent raised an eyebrow.

"Yes and no. They would still be vampires." Travis tried to synthesize what he had read. "The spells don't affect the vampirism, but they do attack their immortality by draining the magic that sustains them and gives them special abilities."

"I can't imagine that would go over well."

"Probably not." Travis stared at the book as if it were a serpent. "And I'm certain that vampires in the Sinistram would have magic."

"If you can remove a vampire's immortality, couldn't you do the same to any other immortal?"

"There doesn't appear to be anything here that deals with the others, only vampires. Maybe only if the immortality was acquired, not natural. Like it wouldn't kill a demigod, but it would affect someone who started off human. There could be multiple reasons the book was hidden," Travis said.

"If all that is possible, why haven't we heard of people doing it?" Brent asked.

"Magic always comes with a cost," Travis replied. "There are the risks of using power for the caster and anyone who isn't the target, and then there's the price to be paid for using tainted magic."

"What kind of cost?" Brent's voice had gone flat, worry clear in his eyes. "Drain your life force? Forfeit your own magic? Corrupt your soul? Have you dragged to Hell by demons?"

"I'm just reading that part," Travis admitted. While he feared that the penalty might indeed be that high, he hoped he could find a second way.

"You're researching on the Dark Web and considering spells from forbidden texts," Brent pointed out. "There are good reasons those sources are disavowed."

"You were in the Army," Travis replied. "You're familiar with the escalation of force. At the upper end, when the threat is severe, the options are limited and come with significant downsides."

"I'm not sure I'd call nuclear annihilation a downside, but I get what you're saying," Brent admitted. "We need to consult with Father Jacinski. Even if he hasn't studied that particular book, maybe he has some insight into how you can work the magic and still survive."

"That's a good idea."

"You look like you need a break," Brent said.

"We don't have time—"

"If you push yourself until you collapse, it will take longer than if you stop for some sugar and caffeine," Brent reasoned. "It's pretty obvious that everything you're doing is taking a toll."

Travis gave up arguing. He stepped out of the circle, and Brent refreshed his coffee and shoved a plate of cookies into his hands. Despite the urgency of the situation, Travis knew Brent was right. Powerful spells were taxing to read, a built-in precaution. Travis already felt a headache starting. He always thought of the effects as being a way the writers screened for those strong enough to handle the magic.

"When we're ready to go, I thought about calling CHARON and telling them that we're going up against the ones who murdered Shane," Brent said. "They won't give a damn if vampires want to kill me, but they might want to avenge him."

"Do you think CHARON's been compromised like the Sinistram? We don't want to give away the plan."

"Shane didn't seem to think so. But we can table that and see if we need reinforcements," Brent acknowledged.

Travis called Jacinski, who answered on the second ring. "Travis? What's wrong? You don't make social calls."

"What do the Logonje know about a grimoire called the Precepts?"

He could hear Jacinski catch his breath in surprise. "Why do you ask?"

"Because a Keeper stole it from the Sinistram and told me it might be the key to stopping the Apocalypse," Travis replied.

"Okay," Jacinski drew out the syllables of the word. "You have it in your possession?"

"Yes, and I'm working on figuring out what we need to stop the vampires who have taken over the upper echelons of this branch of the Sinistram." Travis figured he might as well get all the crazy out of the way up front.

"Jesus, Travis. You don't do things by halves, do you?"

"Believe me, Pawel, I'd rather be doing pretty much anything else," Travis assured him.

Jacinski was quiet for a moment. "The Logonje are a secretive Order of Polish priests who deal with supernatural threats, much like the Occulatum. We were never quite as convinced of our importance as the Sinistram—no offense meant."

"I know what you mean," Travis replied. "No offense taken."

"I think on some level, the Order always suspected we might end up facing off against the Sinistram," Jacinski said. "But maybe not over the Apocalypse."

Travis and Brent took turns filling him in on what they had learned.

"We have the who: Sinistram. And the what: bring about the End of Days," Brent said.

"And we know the why," Travis added. "Because the Sinistram trained and prepared for the Apocalypse and felt cheated when it didn't happen, so they decided to bring it about themselves."

"Fuck," Jacinski muttered.

"We also have a good idea of the how: massive explosions," Brent added.

"And the where: Moraine State Park, although it could spread to other locations."

"Do you know when?" Jacinski asked.

"Soon. Next couple of days at the most," Travis said. "Is there an auspicious date coming up?"

"A full moon. No special ritual dates," Jacinski replied.

"I think the answer to stopping the Sinistram is in the volume the Keeper brought me. If I can figure out the spell, I'll need backup magic to work them and keep everyone else safe. Would you join us? Are there any others you'd trust to come along?"

Travis crossed his fingers. He had doubts about his own magic being sufficient to cast the spell, but having other witches around to lend him power and protect the area made the odds of success much higher.

"Yes, I will. And I'll make some calls to folks I trust in the Logonje and Father Leo with the Occulatum," Jacinski said. "The Sinistram isn't going to ignore this. Are you prepared for that?"

Travis gave a bitter chuckle. "Honestly? I don't know. From what the Keeper said, there's discord in the ranks about turning the place over to vampires. That alone is huge because the Sinistram doesn't tolerate differences of opinion. But at least some of the priests think their whole mission and history have been betrayed."

"Because they have been," Jacinski replied. "And there's no way to know whether those people will be with you or against you, no matter how strong their feelings."

"I understand. But we have to do something," Travis said. "We think that the vampire elders have been behind the hunter deaths that have escalated recently, and that they've used magic to power up monsters like the Mon River creature and others to draw out the hunters and make them easy targets."

"There's always a price for magic," Jacinski warned. "Have you factored that into your plans?"

Brent looked at Travis with worry, but Travis nodded with a certainty that didn't quite reach his gut. "Yes, if that's what it takes. We can't let them bring about the end of the world, even if it's a local apocalypse instead of a global one."

"What's your next move?" Jacinski asked.

"We're waiting to hear from a couple of other friends with special talents who are rallying the troops." Travis left out that one of those friends was a vampire himself. "Then we show up to work the magic, which might precipitate the 'When.' Someone's got to make the first move."

Saying that made him sick to his stomach, not wanting to be the one who started the End of Days. But at the same time, forcing a confrontation might be their only chance to draw Sinistram out on their own terms.

"Yeah, that makes sense," Jacinski said. "Let me check in with a few people I trust and call you back. I'm guessing you aren't planning to get to sleep anytime soon?"

"No, not soon." *And maybe never again.*

"The situation sucks, but thanks for trusting me and calling me in," Jacinski said. "Maybe this is the moment we all ultimately trained for, even if we didn't know it. Who knows? Someone might write a song about us."

He ended the call, and Travis looked to Brent. "I guess it would be cheesy to roar into the park blaring a soundtrack of songs about the apocalypse."

Brent chuckled. "Can't say I'd mind, but that sort of thing probably only works in movies."

Travis went back to working on the grimoire, while Brent returned to researching on his laptop. When Travis's phone rang, he realized it was midnight already.

"Cassidy and Sorren, thanks for calling back. Do you want to go with your news first or ours?"

"I'll start," Sorren said. "Archibald Donnelly and Rowan are with us. We have other allies who plan to work supportive magic remotely," Sorren told them. "They are researching spells and protections and can meet you when you have a when and where."

Travis cleared his throat. "About that. We've figured out the who, what, why, how, and where, and we think the when is the full moon tomorrow night." He filled Sorren in on what they had learned.

"But we also got an unexpected gift," he added. "One of the Keepers from the Sinistram secret library dropped off the Precepts grimoire."

Sorren was silent for a moment. "You're sure."

"Positive."

"It was rumored that the Sinistram had it, but we weren't certain," Sorren said. "Do you understand what the book is and how dangerous it can be? Not just to my kind, but to you, to people with magic, and to supernatural creatures? Can you read it?"

"So far, yes, I can read it. And I'm getting a growing idea of the danger," Travis replied. "From what I've read so far, the Precepts grimoire is connected by its author to the Sinistram, so only someone with a Sinistram connection can use it."

"But you left the Sinistram," Brent said.

Travis sighed. "Not according to them. That whole bit about 'thou art a priest forever.'"

"Do you think you're strong enough to work the magic?" Sorren asked.

Travis took a deep breath. "I think I'm going to have to be. I'm the only one of us who used to be Sinistram. Pawel Jacinski is reaching out to the Logonje and the Occulatum for help, and we have some less powerful witches who can secure the perimeter."

"Good. We will need all that help." Sorren paused. "I can't believe we're talking about the Precepts. It's legendary among my kind. Or perhaps, more like the boogeymen. Many people doubted it still existed, or that it ever did. Fitting, I guess, for the End of Days."

"How do we use it and not hurt the good witches, vampires, and immortals?" Travis asked.

"No spell is powerful enough to work its effects worldwide," Sorren replied. "Look for an indication of the magic's reach. It's going to take enough out of the caster to affect a limited area close by."

"How many people are part of the Sinistram? Do you think they'll all show up to fight?" Brent asked.

Travis did some mental calculations and grimaced. "When I was still part of the group, there were seven elders, possibly two dozen lower-level priests like me, and probably five or six Keepers, who never left the library.

"As for whether they'll all show up, I can't imagine the Keepers coming, but then again, I didn't expect one to appear on my doorstep," Travis said. "As for the others, we worked in small strike groups. Even for large threats, that was usually sufficient."

"Would the regular priests fight to defend vampires?" Brent put into words something Travis had wondered.

"Under regular circumstances, no. But clearly things have changed. I don't think the elders could have turned all of the priests, or there would be no one left to say the Sacraments and handle the types of missions we undertook." Travis grimaced when he realized he had included himself with "we."

"I don't know how far their loyalty goes," Travis admitted. "I'm hoping that the Precepts spell can be limited to affecting just vampires, not everyone with abilities."

"We've also got the Logonje and Occulatum on our side," Brent pointed out. "And possibly CHARON."

"Can we trust CHARON?" Sorren asked.

"Hell, no," Brent said. "But if the 'enemy of my enemy is my friend' and the Sinistram ordered Shane's murder, then I think they could play a role. I still wouldn't tell them anything until the last minute, just in case. But they'd be an asset if they came."

Sorren paused. "Do you understand the cost?"

"Probably not completely," Travis admitted, and Brent glared at him. "I figured I have a lot of studying ahead of me tonight."

"I will see what Donnelly knows, and I would suggest you work closely with Jacinski and Leo," Sorren told him. "At the least, I'd expect the spell to draw from your energy, maybe even your soul. You'll need to make sure that you have witches nearby who can replenish you and tether your soul to your body. This is big magic, but don't assume it requires you to sacrifice your life to save the world."

"We'll also have Dr. Peters with us, if it comes to keeping soul and body together," Travis replied, reminding Sorren of their necromancer friend.

"As well as Rowan and Archibald Donnelly," Sorren added. "Although it's probably best I remain in Charleston, for obvious reasons."

Travis didn't mention the visions he had seen over the last twelve hours, watching the different possibilities play out. Sometimes they won, defeating the elders and stopping Sinistram. In others, the whole park went up in a fireball and them with it. No version seemed more likely than another, which is why he hadn't told Brent about the dreams.

The longer Travis studied the Precepts, the more he felt its drain on his energy. He understood the concept of an unholy bargain, and while he was willing to sacrifice himself, if necessary, to stop the Sinistram apocalypse, he desperately hoped there would be a way that didn't drain him dry in the process.

"Thank you," Travis replied, although he knew he wouldn't be completely reassured until they had figured out how the final battle would go down. "I'd like to stick around."

CHAPTER TEN

"COVENS, take the lake shore, and make sure you cover the cemeteries and the spots near where the towns were flooded," Brent told the witches. "Do your best to keep anyone from exploding the oil and gas wells. You'll also be protecting Travis and lending him whatever power you can spare.

"Pre-cogs and mediums, stay back from the front lines but keep your phones on and let me know if anything changes," he added. "The ghosts are our eyes and ears. Use them as scouts to keep from getting surprised."

Rowan and Aricella had gathered and briefed the witches earlier that day, ensuring everyone knew the needed spells and understood their role of keeping supernatural attackers at bay. The two more powerful witches intended to stay with Travis and Brent, as did Archibald Donnelly and Dr. Peters, figuring that necromancy would be the most help in keeping the restless dead at bay.

Jacinski and the half-dozen Logonje priests chose to cover the most haunted spots, the ones that might pose the greatest threat as the lake's dark magic powered up. Father Leo and the six Occulatum priests went with them. They were already in position.

"I don't like doing this at night," Travis grumbled. "Vampires sleep during the day."

"We weren't going to get far in daylight, not with park visitors and security," Brent reminded him.

"I know. But I don't have to like it."

Brent stayed with Travis, backing him up with guns and his limited ability to see ghosts. They had chosen the spot closest to where the town of Mayne had been flooded, marked by stone pillars, railroad tracks that led nowhere, and an overgrown cemetery.

Some of the allied covens were on alert for attack, protecting the ritual area as best they could, given the large size of the park. Others laid down suppressing magic to avoid having the old gas and oil wells explode.

"Do you think the elders know we're here?" Travis asked as he got the final elements ready for the ritual.

"If they don't yet, they will soon," Brent said.

"What are the odds that CHARON will show up?"

"Guess we'll find out," Brent replied.

An hour ago, taking travel time from Pittsburgh into consideration, Brent had forced himself to make the phone call.

"Lawson? What the hell do you want?" a voice Brent recognized as Clark Davis answered.

"Shut up and listen. The Sinistram elders have been turned. They're vampires now. We're doing a ritual at Moraine State Park in an hour to stop them. You want in?"

"If this is your idea of a joke—"

"In or out? The magic is starting."

"We'll be there." Davis ended the call.

"If they left right after my call, they should be getting here any minute. And if they did betray us to the Sinistram, they didn't give them much of a heads up." Brent glanced at his watch, then looked at Travis. "It's time to start the party."

Brent watched Travis take a few deep breaths to clear his mind. Rowan and Aricella had already created a warded circle for them and raised a dome of protective magic to keep him from being interrupted by magic or spirits. A lit candle was placed within reach.

Travis wore a silver crucifix, several saints' medallions, and had a flask of salted holy water. Brent also wore charms and amulets, along with protective hex bags. Given the powerful magic to be worked, those talismans couldn't save them from a full blast, but Brent took comfort from them and figured every little bit helped.

Travis opened the steel case and pulled on magically neutral gloves made of a fine silver mesh before he lifted the Precepts grimoire from its resting place.

"Even with the gloves, I can feel the book's magic, tugging at me. It's like the power of the lake—so strong," Travis told him. "The energy goes deep down, and it's very, very old." He pulled out a couple glow sticks and snapped them. They'd add enough light to what the candle provided for him to read, but wouldn't distract the others.

"The ghosts are paying attention," Brent added. "They're awake and watching. Curious and skeptical. Here's hoping they take our side."

"Here I go. Wish me luck." With that, Travis began to speak the Latin incantation that Brent knew his partner had silently rehearsed but dared not say aloud before now. Even with his limited abilities, Brent could sense the ancient magic and thought it felt stained and twisted.

A ritual of this power and magnitude took time, and Brent sensed the spell seeping into the land beneath their feet and into their bones, and perhaps into their souls. He felt the strength in the language used, the dark poetry of the phrasing, the cadence of its consonants like clacking bones.

An icy wind swept past as even more spirits gathered, long overdue for rest and justice.

"I call on the power of the lake and the deep places. Scour the rot of undeath away from the elders of the Sinistram and strip away their unholy magic," Travis said.

Travis looked down at a yellowed piece of parchment, even more discolored in the glow. The Investiture Certificate had been presented to him when he was taken into the Sinistram as a novitiate long ago. Brent had feared that Travis might have gotten rid of it in a fit of pique after he left the Order and felt relief when his friend discovered it in his desk.

There was nothing magical about the certificate itself, but as part of the ceremony, each of the Sinistram elders had signed the paper. He had their names and their signatures. That gave him power.

Travis took a deep breath and began to read aloud.

"Enzo Bianchi, Luciano Cattaneo, Giuseppe Sala, Pietro Lombardi, Elia Bonfante, Cosimo Fanucci, Ludovic Dugoni, you have betrayed your vows, betrayed the purpose of the Order, and sold your souls for the dark magic of the undead.

"I renounce your betrayal, and by all that is Holy, renounce the abhorrent power that has consumed you." Travis switched to Latin for the next part of the rite, while he carried out the other elements of the spell.

He took a pinch of specially-mixed herbs and dropped them into the candle flame, watching the fire turn colors and send sparks into the air. As he chanted, he drew flaming sigils in the air. Brent felt the tug of the magic on his energy, and perhaps on his soul, deep within.

The air shimmered, a swell of power made Brent's head ache like a coming thunderstorm, and then seven men stood at a distance from where he and Travis set up the ritual.

"Travis Dominick," a tall, thin man with sharp features, called out. Brent recognized him as Pietro Lombardi from Travis's earlier description. "Stop this charade immediately."

Travis never hesitated, continuing the chant, not even acknowledging the interruption.

Rowan, Aricella, Donnelly, and Peters moved a few steps closer, an unmistakable show of protection.

"This is your last warning. Return to the fold, and all will be forgiven," Lombardi snapped, annoyed at being ignored.

Brent didn't believe him, although he didn't doubt the Sinistram leader would like to have Travis's magic under his control.

"You can't win," Cosimo Fanucci, a short blond man, told them. "Put your toys away and stand down."

If we don't pose a threat, why are they here? Brent felt certain that Travis's plan and the Precepts incantation were just as dangerous as they believed, and the Sinistram elders knew it.

Brent heard Donnelly and Peters murmur quiet words of power. Lombardi laughed in response.

"Your necromancy won't work against our magic," Lombardi told them. "We are no longer mere vampires."

Flashes of light and the clatter of distant fighting drew Brent's attention toward several spots along the edge of the park where he knew the Logonje were stationed. Elsewhere, along one of the moraine mounds, he heard raised voices and saw shimmers in the darkness as power was traded and countered.

"You're too little, too late," Lombardi gloated. "Everything that must happen has already occurred. The wheels are turning. They cannot be stopped."

A dozen black-clad Sinistram priests poured from the shadows, and Brent hoped the Logonje and Occulatum could keep them at bay long enough for Travis to work the spell.

Heavily-armed newcomers dressed in camouflage fatigues burst from beneath the trees and met the Sinistram advance, and Brent knew CHARON had kept their promise.

Ninja-priests clashed with special forces-trained operatives, both sides well-versed in magic. The Sinistram rushed the fighters, chanting spells as they drew their knives.

CHARON opened fire with a small arsenal of weapons. Magic deflected most of the bullets from striking the priests, but the fusillade stopped the Sinistram's advance and forced them to switch from offense to defense.

It's a bit like Mothra vs. Godzilla, Brent thought, firing into the melee whenever he got a clear shot at one of the warrior-priests. For today, at least, CHARON operatives were allies.

He didn't dare lob any of Travis's enhanced flash bangs, given the number of uncapped oil and gas wells just beneath the ground, so he made do by laying down rounds of defensive fire with a semiautomatic rifle to keep the priests away from the spelled dome where Travis worked the incantation.

"You can't prevent what has been foretold!" Fanucci shouted, features animated with anticipation for the grand finale, the end of all things.

"Maybe. Maybe not," Brent countered. "But with the Precepts, we can stop *you*."

"Don't believe the traitor from the library." Lombardi's expression twisted to a snarl. "He has been dealt with." Brent knew he meant the Keeper who had brought Travis the grimoire.

"It begins." Lombardi looked up as a brilliant light streaked across the dark sky, and Brent recognized it as the comet Travis had been tracking.

Momentarily distracted by the comet, Brent realized seconds too late that the elders had used their magic in the brief cease-fire to turn the park itself against Travis and their friends.

Explosions burst across the park's rolling ground as the elders' magic ignited the old wells, spraying dirt high into the air and sending up plumes of flame.

Just like in Travis's vision, Brent thought.

The elders rushed forward, sure of their impending success.

Brent fired enchanted silver rounds as Aricella and Rowan shouted spells to hold back the attackers. Donnelly and Peters moved their hands silently, weaving magic that sent a shiver through Brent.

Whatever the elders had done to regroup, this time they did not fear bullets, and magic only served to slow them, not keep them at bay. Brent didn't know what would happen if they reached the protected dome before Travis finished the incantation, but he feared the worst.

Fog rose from the ground, taking shape as the ghosts of Moraine heeded the call.

A gray army of revenants materialized, rising from their flooded graves and forgotten burying places. Some went for the Sinistram priests while others rushed at the elders, intent on slowing their advance. Brent felt certain he spotted Eagle Eye Ike among them like a general marshalling his troops.

"Cover me," Brent said to Rowan as he reloaded. He spared a second to glance at his partner. Travis looked tired and haggard but kept chanting, as the powerful incantation and dark magic took a toll. Brent knew they were running out of time.

Brent was inside the protective dome, Travis's last defense. Rowan and the others were outside, keeping up a non-stop barrage of magic to keep the elders clear of the warded area. No matter what the witches threw at Lombardi and his fellows, the Sinistram managed to counter. Brent knew the impasse couldn't last and silently urged Travis to hurry.

More explosions shook the ground. So far, the blasts had been at a distance from where Travis worked his magic, but Brent feared for the covens supporting them, and for the CHARON fighters in spite of himself. Deep as their differences went, he had invited them to share in a battle with a common foe, not to get them blown to bits.

The witches can't hide all the explosions. Sooner or later, the cops are going to show up, and if we aren't done with the magic, it will be an utter clusterfuck.

Travis raised his head, looking up from the Precepts. His eyes were bloodshot, and he looked like he hadn't slept in days, but he spoke loudly and with authority as he raised the grimoire and stared through the dome at the elders.

Brent's rifle clicked empty, and he dropped it, out of ammo. He pulled his Glock, exchanging high volume for targeted head shots. A glance at Rowan and the other defenders told him that they couldn't hold the line much longer.

Half a dozen Sinistram priests rushed toward the dome, weapons drawn, chanting spells of their own. Brent fired methodically, downing two of them. Rowan's magic set two priests on fire, while whatever the two necromancers did made the last two priests drop in their tracks as if their hearts suddenly stopped.

Another wave of priests followed them, undeterred by their colleagues' deadly failure. The elders kept their distance, using the rank-and-file Sinistram priests as cannon fodder. He was surprised that many were able to get past CHARON and the others.

"We're running out of time," Brent shouted over his shoulder at Travis. "It's now or never!"

Brent thought he had brought enough ammo for a war, but he had underestimated the opposition. He couldn't keep this up much longer, and his aim wavered from fatigue and adrenaline. Rowan and the other witches forced the Sinistram to retreat, but every time the priests gained a little more ground than they lost. Brent didn't know how much power necromancy took compared to regular magic, but even Donnely and Peters looked near exhaustion. In the distance, he could see the remaining priests battling CHARON, keeping the Sinistram from interfering.

"Sunder the magic from the undead. Walking corpses have no claim to energy and power. As of old, so shall it be now. Revoke!"

Travis repeated the command in Latin, but even before he could finish, Brent felt the buzz of powerful magic fill the dome and lash out beyond toward the vampiric elders. Streaks of blue fire struck each of them in the chest.

Lombardi and Fanucci burst into flame, screaming as their bodies were consumed. Two more caught fire seconds later, while the last three staggered, then fell to the ground, convulsed, and lay still.

Donnelly and Peters ran forward, already speaking binding spells on the weakened vampires. Now that the elders had been stripped of their sustaining magic, they could no longer maintain their spells against the necromancers' power.

Travis lowered the grimoire and staggered. Brent rushed to steady him as Travis tried to stand.

"Eat. Drink. You did it." Brent pressed a bottle of water and a protein bar into Travis's hands.

"Is it over?" Travis's voice sounded scratchy and sore, and utter exhaustion showed in his face.

"Looks like it. De-magicking torched four of them, and the other three are down. Donnelly and Peters have them handled." Brent watched closely to make sure Travis replenished himself. He looked close to collapse, but he stubbornly stayed on his feet.

"The oldest ones burned," Travis croaked. "I guess their immortality and their vampirism got too tangled up to separate. As for the others, no idea whether they'll recover."

With the elders captured or destroyed, the few remaining Sinistram fighters either surrendered or made a break for it. Those who ran were quickly captured by the Logonje and Occulatum, helped by ghosts who revealed their hiding places. Brent guessed that CHARON had moved to secure the perimeter and head off law enforcement.

Rowan and Aricella let the warded dome fall.

"Great job, Travis," Rowan said.

"You did it!" Aricella cheered.

"I'll rally the covens and make sure that the wells that haven't exploded yet, won't," Rowan said.

"And I'll help settle the spirits," Aricella added. She gave Brent a pointed look. "Take care of Travis."

"I wonder how much of a mess there is," Brent mused, unable to see far in the dark. He had no idea how many of the capped wells had exploded, but he could imagine the damage caused to what had been a stretch of green lawn.

"Less than the end of the world," Travis remarked. He sat down on a log, and Brent tried not to hover but stayed close by. Travis finished the water and food, handing back the empty bottle and wrapper.

"That helped, thank you. But I could sleep for a week, drink a couple gallons of water, and eat a dozen double-cheeseburgers, not necessarily in that order." Travis managed a tired smile. Brent thought he already looked a bit improved, but didn't doubt that time, sleep, and food would speed the recovery.

———

JUST AFTER DAWN, the hum of rotors overhead made Brent look up. "What the fuck?"

A Chinook helicopter hovered overhead. "Clear for landing," an Italian-accented voice said from a loudspeaker.

Brent, Travis, and the remaining fighters on the field drew back, but kept both arcane and regular weapons in hand.

The helicopter landed, and the hatch opened. A dozen men in European-cut business suits disembarked, and their leader approached Brent and Travis, brandishing a badge and carrying a stainless-steel briefcase.

"Who the hell are you?" Brent demanded as he examined the credentials. He also noticed the man's holstered Sig Saur P220.

"Supernatural Swiss Guard," the man replied in Italian-accented English, unperturbed by Brent's tone. "I am Lieutenant Colonel Vincente Rosso. We're here to take the troublemakers to the Vatican, where they will be judged and suitably punished."

Brent had heard of the Swiss Guard, the protectors of the Pope, but usually saw pictures of them in traditional regalia and hadn't considered that they had a supernatural branch, or that they could dress like a modern security detail.

"We could have used you last night, when we were fighting for our lives," Travis snapped.

"You didn't ask for our help," Rosso replied, as his companions spread out and began to gather the downed and dead Sinistram members.

"I wasn't in the mood for praying," Travis returned.

"We have a phone number," Lieutenant Colonel Rosso remarked in a dry tone.

"You came all the way from Rome in a helicopter?" Travis asked.

Rosso shook his head. "Took a jet to the nearest airport, and a helicopter from there. Those hover planes are only in the movies, unfortunately."

"How did you know what was going on or where we were?" Travis asked.

Rosso gave an enigmatic smile. "We were notified by the Keepers."

"What will happen to the elders and the other Sinistram priests?" Brent was going to have to think through the role of the Keepers later, when the adrenaline had time to settle.

"That's for the Holy Father to decide," Rosso replied. "The survivors will be tried, defrocked, and detained indefinitely. They will no longer pose a danger."

"What about the Pittsburgh chapter of the Sinistram?" Travis asked, and Brent could tell his friend was doing his best to rein in his temper. They were both exhausted and wounded, and the adrenaline of the life-or-death fight was just starting to wane.

"A thorough investigation will be made," Rosso assured them. Behind him, the guards escorted cuffed and muzzled elders and Sinistram priests to the helicopter, and carried the dead on litters.

"The situation is...unprecedented," Rosso replied. "The tribunal will interview the membership, weigh the evidence, and make a determination. Until then, the chapter and the library will be on lockdown, under the protection of the Keepers."

Rosso looked at the Precepts volume in Travis's hands. "I'm not sure how you got that, but it belongs to the Sinistram."

"It was given to me by one of the Keepers who wanted to stop what was going on," Travis replied. "Thanks to him, we were able to avert a major disaster."

"Just to be clear, they intended to bring about the Apocalypse, the End of Days," Brent interjected. "They were all prepared and tired of waiting, so they thought they'd wipe the slate clean and start over."

Russo's discomfort was clear, despite his professional demeanor. "We've been made aware." He looked suitably abashed. "I regret that you and your friends were endangered. We are in your debt, and I promise that we will investigate how the chapter hid its changes from us so completely."

He cleared his throat. "But I must insist on the return of the Precepts."

Travis hesitated, and Brent could guess his conflict. They had only the reputation of the Swiss Guard to vouch for its integrity, but the tome clearly wasn't safe with the Sinistram, and Brent couldn't imagine that any of the other organizations they worked with could provide as high security as the guards.

After a moment, Travis placed the grimoire in the briefcase, which Brent saw was etched with protective sigils and runes.

"Keep it out of the wrong hands," Travis said, with a pointed look at Russo.

Brent wondered whether the Occulatum or the Logonje had also gotten word to the Vatican. Despite their assistance with the grimoire, he struggled to imagine the Keepers ratting out their superiors to the Holy See.

In minutes, the Swiss Guard had loaded their prisoners aboard the helicopter.

"You have the thanks and blessing of the Holy Father," Russo told them. "I hope our paths need not cross again." He strode back to the helicopter, which lifted off as soon as he was aboard.

"I kinda wish they had shown up in those striped outfits with the puffy sleeves and the halberds," Brent said as they watched the helicopter fly away.

"I was disappointed when I found out that they have modern weapons, even machine guns." Travis looked toward the departing helicopter in the sky. "I don't know how that's escaped notice by video game creators."

"People don't worry much about sacrilege these days, but that might be a bit over the top," Brent replied.

"Probably so." Travis looked across the field as a man strode toward them. "Head's up. Your CHARON person is heading our way."

"He's not *my* person," Brent grumbled.

The guy looked like ex-military, with a muscular build. He wore a black shirt and pants clearly inspired by special ops. Brent knew him as Clark Davis, but he doubted that was the man's real name.

"Lawson. You called. We came to avenge Shane. Remember that when you're thinking of how much you hate us," Davis said.

"Thanks for the assist, but you stood as much to lose as the rest of us," Brent reminded him. "I gave you a heads-up on self-preservation, for CHARON and the whole city. Protecting civilians from supernatural threats was the mission, at least the last time you tried to recruit me."

Davis looked like he had a bad taste in his mouth. "That hasn't changed. Who were your buddies with the fancy helicopter? CIA? FBI?"

"Vatican." Brent took satisfaction from the surprise in the other man's eyes. "Swiss Guard."

Davis covered his shock quickly. "Just remember you asked for help, and we came when you called. You could still join us."

"Stopping the End of Days doesn't count as a personal favor, since the alternative is exterminating mankind," Brent observed. "You had some skin in the game."

"Remember what I said," Davis replied, choosing to ignore the barb.

He turned away and headed toward where he and the other CHARON agents had presumably left their black SUVs, disappearing into the shadows.

"Kinda makes me sorry we didn't blow up any of the wells where he parked," Travis said in an off-handed tone that made Brent chuckle despite Davis's high-handedness.

"We definitely missed an opportunity," Brent replied.

"Hey. The guy is a douchebag. He's probably pissed that the

Apocalypse was going to happen, and he had no clue, had to hear it from you. That's gotta sting," Travis said.

"Yeah, I guess so." Brent looked out over the moon-lit field that their allies had now cleared of bodies and arcane evidence. The witches had made good on their promise to keep mundane authorities away, but Brent knew that wouldn't last forever.

"We should get going. I don't want to end up downtown answering the cops' questions." Brent knew the witches gave them as much magical cover as possible, but it would be hard to miss the explosions.

"Now that we've shut down the elders, do you think the old ones and the other supernatural trouble they stirred up will go away?" Brent asked.

Travis shrugged. "No way to know. Probably, although no idea how fast. Might take a while. If the old ones have been here all along, then they've come and gone more than once over the centuries. But it should stop the attacks on hunters, and that counts for a lot."

When they got back to Brent's house, Travis insisted that they do a thorough check to ensure there were no lurking threats.

"I'm officially proclaiming us on vacation for a couple of weeks," Brent told him. "Someone else can save the world. We deserve a break, at least, for a while."

Travis chuckled. "I'm not sure it works that way, but I'm all for the idea. Get some sleep."

Brent lightly thumped the roof of the Crown Vic in goodbye and walked into the house. Thanks to timers, the lights were on, and it didn't seem quite so long since he had been home.

"Glad you're back," Brent said when he saw Danny's ghost sitting on the couch. He wondered how long his brother had waited for him to return. Brent poured himself some whiskey and sat down across from Danny.

"I'm glad you're safe. It was a good thing you weren't with us at the park. That was...pretty bad."

Danny looked at him with concern.

"I'm a little sore, but nothing dangerous. Got lucky."

Danny put his hand over his heart, and Brent could guess his meaning. *I love you. Be safe. Don't be in a hurry to catch up to me.*

"The ghosts were badass. They ran interference and helped keep the bad guys from doing even more damage. I hope they can rest easier now." Brent had questions for Donnelly or Dr. Peters if he ever had a chance to talk with the necromancers. He was grateful for the help ghosts often lent them during battles, but he also hoped they weren't harming the spirits by draining their energy or pulling them back into earthly conflicts.

Danny shot him the bratty smirk Brent missed so much. He knew Danny was telling him not to worry so much. Brent was surprised that, even after years separated by death, Danny still knew him better than anyone.

"I'll try not to overthink it. Guess I never did have a poker face. The ghosts who showed up to help wanted to be there. Maybe they were working off unfinished business. Or maybe they just wanted to feel a little closer to the living."

"We might have saved the world tonight. Or at least, a corner of it. I hope we can go back to busting bad witches, low-level demons, and poltergeists and leave the Apocalypse to those guys in the movies," Brent told Danny.

Brent's head throbbed, and now that the adrenaline high had worn off, he felt the fight in every joint and sinew. He didn't expect the whiskey to do more than take the edge off, but even that was an improvement.

Danny mimed clasping his hands and swooning. Brent knew he meant "you're still my hero." Brent felt his cheeks heat in a way that had nothing to do with the whiskey. "Just doin' my job."

Brent knocked back the last of his drink. "Thanks for stopping in. Don't be a stranger."

Danny's form wavered. He waved goodbye before his apparition vanished.

Brent set his glass aside and got up from his chair with a grunt as sore muscles protested every move. He knew they had been lucky to escape with so few injuries and win their fight without losing anyone on their side. Still, there had been moments when it had been by the skin of their teeth, and he knew it could easily have gone wrong so many times.

We survived. Lived to fight another day. That's as good as it gets. I'm going to take the win and try to sleep it off.

CHAPTER ELEVEN

A WEEK LATER, Brent and Travis met up with Mark Wojcik and Father Leo at Fletcher's Bar outside Conneaut Lake.

"Thank you again for bringing in the Occulatum," Travis told Father Leo. "They were a big help."

"You're very welcome. It's been a while since we've worked with Father Jacinski and the Logonje," Leo replied. "Nice to see everyone assemble for a good cause."

Brent chuckled. "Not exactly the Avengers."

Leo shrugged. "Close enough. And that Vatican helicopter was snazzy."

"I think that's one party I'm glad I skipped," Mark said, after a long drink of his coffee. "But ever since your get-together at Moraine, there haven't been any more hunter hits. The monsters have calmed down to normal levels. Whatever passes for normal for us, anyhow."

"Good to know," Travis replied.

"Did you ever find out how the authorities explained the explosions?" Mark asked.

Brent shrugged. "There was a promise that the wells would be screened, new safety measures would be implemented, blah, blah,

blah. As for why things went boom, I heard it was blamed on a rogue discharge of static electricity," he added with a smirk.

"The witches did a damn good job of keeping the authorities away during the fight and covering up the mess afterward," Travis said. "We had agreed on an exit route ahead of time, so that's where everyone parked, and the magic kept it hidden long enough for us to get out. It helped that the Swiss Guard took the bodies."

"In a backhanded way, this whole shitfest probably strengthened hunter alliances," Mark added. "We're usually a curmudgeonly pack of loners, but at least for now, I'm seeing hunters do better asking for backup and sharing tips. I don't know if it'll last, but it's progress."

"CHARON's back to being the same old arrogant sons-of-bitches they usually are," Brent said. "Davis thought this whole mess might get me to change my mind. I made it clear it didn't."

"The Sinistram is on lockdown until the Vatican cleans up the mess," Travis added. "While I wouldn't normally care, it also means the library is closed. And after everything that happened, I'll never look at the Keepers quite the same way again."

"Do you think other chapters will heed the warning?" Mark asked.

"I suspect that the Holy Father will get his point across sternly," Travis replied with a bitter chuckle. "But I don't expect the replacement elders to be any more ethical than their predecessors, even if they are mortal. Although at this point, I strongly doubt they'll keep trying to get me back into the fold after the role I played in the regime change."

"The Logonje and the Occulatum will remain on alert, now that we know what threat to watch for," Father Leo said. "We forgot that the most dangerous monsters are human."

"Whatever the elders did that woke up the old ones has faded," Brent told them. "No more Messie in the Mon, the mine monsters are quiet, and the dark power at Lake Arthur is silent. I'm hoping that any other vampires or powerful immortals out there will decide that trying to take over isn't worth it."

"Long overdue, but now that we've realized the potential threat from all the capped wells, some of our witch friends reinforced the protective spell from the battle so it stays in place to prevent future explosions," Travis added. "And we'll be on the lookout for other spots like that, so maybe we can prevent the next apocalypse."

"How are you two?" Father Leo asked. "My priests and I managed to avoid most of the hand-to-hand fighting, but the magical drain was pretty severe. I didn't want to get out of bed for days, and I know I won't be back to full magic for a while yet."

Brent intentionally didn't look at Travis, leaving it up to his partner to divulge the price of using the dark magic of the Precepts. "My bruises have bruises, and my sore muscles are reminding me that I'm not as young as I was in my Army days." Brent stretched ruefully.

"I'm healing." Travis looked at his drink. "One day at a time, from the inside out. I'm still a little untethered, which is weird, but I'm working on that. Father Jacinski hooked me up with a Logonje priest who also does post-battle magical injury therapy, and it's helping."

"Don't be ashamed of asking for help," Father Leo said. "I'm glad you've found resources. And your friends are here when you need us."

"Thank you," Travis looked a bit sheepish at admitting his injuries.

Brent kept in touch with Jon and Matthew to support Travis as he recovered, sourcing help from their witch friends, brujas, and healers as the need arose. Travis didn't confide much, even to them, but he knew from Jon and Matthew how often Travis woke screaming or stayed up all night. Fortunately, those incidents seemed to be getting less frequent.

The conversation shifted to less dire subjects, from the weather to the Steelers to television shows and movies. After a while, they settled the bill and walked out together to their cars.

"Don't be strangers." Mark gave each of them a handshake and a firm clap on the back. "The world doesn't have to be ending."

"Same here," Brent replied.

Father Leo blessed them and gave parting hugs. "Call if you need us. Or if you just want to talk." He looked at Travis with the last comment.

"Will do," Travis assured them.

For a while, they drove back to Pittsburgh in silence. Brent listened to the rumble of the Crown Vic's engine and watched the scenery go by.

"How are you, really?" he asked, careful not to make eye contact.

Travis shrugged, uncomfortable despite how close their friendship had become. "They warn about dark magic for good reasons. My counselor said that soul wounds are real, and the source of a person's abilities can be bruised, for lack of a better word. Those take longer to heal than anything physical."

Brent nodded. "Makes sense. And it also explains why people who gravitate to tainted magic end up losing their way and going Dark Side. Slippery slope and all that. It certainly works that way for unethical decisions, even for people without abilities."

"I don't know that I'll ever be sorry for doing it," Travis said, "given what was at stake. And I know that can lead to rationalizing using that kind of power again, for the next dire situation. Which is why I'm glad I have good friends to keep me on the straight-and-narrow."

Brent grinned at him, pleased that Travis had been so candid. "We're going to do our fucking best."

"I'm counting on it."

AUTHOR NOTES

Research is one of my great joys, and it provides so many plot bunnies! Many of the incidents in the book came from real history, although some have had the actual names of the people, places, and companies altered.

The cement factory tragedy was real (although I changed the name), as was the gas company explosion and the mine disasters. Man-made lakes often involve flooding areas with abandoned towns. In most cases, the buildings are destroyed, although stonework and foundations may remain. Headstones are frequently removed from cemeteries, but the bodies are rarely relocated. The old amusement park beneath the lake is also real. The towns mentioned as being flooded by the Lake Arthur project are real, and some ruins remain on the lakeshore.

I've mentioned before that hundreds of miles of abandoned coal mines run beneath this corner of Pennsylvania, and no one has a complete map of their location. Abandoned gas and oil wells are also a real issue. While the state has identified approximately 27,000 of these wells, the Kleinman Center for Energy Policy estimates the true number to be between 300,000 – 750,000. Moraine State Park is estimated to have around 400 such capped wells, as well as more than 50 sealed shaft or slope coal mines.

I didn't make up the missile silos, either. Several abandoned silos exist in the Pittsburgh region, as well as over 100 decommissioned munitions and jet engine testing bunkers. Warheads and weapons have been removed, but the sites remain. The Raven Rock underground nuclear bunker is still active. A remarkable amount of information about the sites is available free online.

The Beaver Valley Nuclear Power Station is operational and is located in Shippingport, which is about thirty miles from Pittsburgh.

The circus train wreck was based on a real event, although I changed the name of the circus. And there really are towns in Northwestern Pennsylvania that were places for retired performers or those wintering over between travel seasons.

Eagle Eye Ike is based on the legend of Loop Hill Ike, a ghost who protects people from other ghosts. Several books dedicated to Ike's legend have been written by area locals.

If you're curious about the old steam engines, there are festivals throughout the summer and fall that showcase these amazing machines. My dad used to collect them, so I had plenty of personal experience with both the shows and the machinery. They are really loud! They are also massive and solid, mighty remnants from a long-ago era.

Truth is stranger than fiction! I love to weave in history and lore from the area where a book is set. Not only does the research give me ideas, but reality often serves up weirder stuff than even my fevered imagination.

ABOUT THE AUTHOR

Gail Z. Martin writes urban fantasy, epic fantasy, and steampunk for Orbit Books, Falstaff Books, SOL Publishing, and Darkwind Press. Urban fantasy series include *Deadly Curiosities* and the *Night Vigil*. Epic fantasy series include *Darkhurst, The Chronicles of The Necromancer, The Fallen Kings Cycle, The Ascendant Kingdoms Saga, and The Assassins of Landria*. Under her urban fantasy MM paranormal romance pen name of Morgan Brice, she has six series (*Witchbane, Badlands, Kings of the Mountain, Fox Hollow, Treasure Trail,* and *Sharps and Springfield*) with more books and series to come.

Co-authored with Larry N. Martin are the Jake Desmet Adventures and the *Storm and Fury* collection; and the *Spells, Salt, & Steel*: New Templars series (Mark Wojcik, monster hunter) as well as the *Wasteland Marshals* series and *The Joe Mack Adventures*.

Gail's work has appeared in more than fifty US/UK anthologies. Newest anthologies include: *The Weird Wild West, Gaslight and Grimm, Baker Street Irregulars, Across the Universe, Release the Virgins, Witches, Warriors, & Wise Women, The Four ???? of the Apocalypse, Nevermore, Three Time Travelers,* and *Solar Flare*.

Join the Shadow Alliance street team so you never miss a new release! Get the scoop first + giveaways + fun stuff! Also where Gail and Larry get their beta readers and Launch Team! http://www.facebook.com/groups/MartinShadowAlliance

Join the newsletter and get free excerpts at http://eepurl.com/dd5XLj Gail is also a con-runner for ConTinual, the online, ongoing

multi-genre convention that never ends. <u>www.Facebook.-</u>
<u>com/Groups/ConTinual</u>

Support Indie Authors

When you support independent authors, you help influence what kind of books you'll see more of and what types of stories will be available because the authors themselves decide which books to write, not a big publishing conglomerate. Independent authors are local creators, supporting their families with the books they produce. Thank you for supporting independent authors and small press fiction!

Tangled Web

Inheritance

Legacy

Tapestry

Trifles and Folly: Collection

Trifles and Folly 2: Collection

Trifles and Folly 3: Collection

Assassins of Landria

Assassin's Honor

Sellsword's Oath

Fugitive's Vow

Exile's Quest

Outlaw's Vengeance

Dead Man's Justice

Night Vigil

Sons of Darkness

C.H.A.R.O.N.

Sinistram

Other books by Gail Z. Martin and Larry N. Martin

Jake Desmet Adventures

Iron & Blood

Spark of Destiny

Storm & Fury: Collection

Spells, Salt, & Steel: New Templars

Spells, Salt, & Steel: Season One

Spells, Salt, & Steel: Season Two

Dead of Winter, Novella #9

Wasteland Marshals

Wasteland Marshals Volume One

Joe Mack: Shadow Council Archives

Forged: Joe Mack Adventures Volume One

Times Change, Novella #5